For all the readers who have journeyed with the
Secret Breakers on their adventures
and in memory of three incredible code-crackers:
Alan Turing, William and Elizebeth Friedman
and all those who worked at Station X.
Finally, thank you to Wilfred Voynich
for finding the most mysterious manuscript
in the world!

# SECRET BREAKERS

## CIRCLE OF FIRE

### H. L. Dennis

Illustrations by Meggie Dennis

Hodder
Children's
Books

A division of Hachette Children's Books

*We shall not cease from exploration*
*And the end of all our exploring*
*Will be to arrive where we started*
*And know the place for the first time.*

*. . . And all shall be well and*
*All manner of thing shall be well*
*When the tongues of flame are infolded*
*Into the crowned knot of fire*
*And the fire and the rose are one.*

**T. S. Eliot, *Four Quartets***

# Escaping the Shadow
# of the
# Blue Ridge Mountains

The Director of Level Five of the British Black Chamber could still smell fire. This made him happy. He could still hear the blades of the windmill as they whipped the air with flame. The memory made the room spin.

He reached for his drink. The bar seemed far away and it took a while to grip the glass. And the room went on spinning. Odd that.

He loosened his tie and undid his top button. His neck throbbed and when he took his hand away the tips of his fingers were wet with sweat. Yet he felt cold. In fact he was shivering.

'You all right, mate?' The bartender was wiping the counter and the sound was excruciatingly loud. The

1

Director looked up. He could see the bartender through the prism of the glass. There seemed to be lots of him, swirling and dancing, and the noise was getting louder. And the smell of the smoke was overwhelming now.

The Director leant forward. His drink slipped from his grasp.

'Mate, seriously? You don't look right.'

But the Director was always right. It was his job to be right. And he tried hard to concentrate on this thought as he fell from the bar stool and hit the ground. Shards of broken glass cut into his face and the last thing he saw before he closed his eyes was his own blood pooling with his spilt drink on the floor.

Kitty McCloud paid the cab driver then he waved her towards the entrance of a shabby hotel across the road.

The receptionist looked up from her paperwork. She wore a practised smile and pushed the chewing gum into the side of her mouth. 'Can I help you?'

'A room for the night, please. And I need it to have a phone.'

The receptionist pulled a face, registering Kitty's accent. 'No international calls from the room. There's a pay-phone there.'

Kitty signed the check-in details and took the key

she was offered. Once inside the small telephone booth beside the desk she emptied all the coins she had into the change tray. Then she took a folded card from her wallet. She didn't really need to check the number – she'd dialled it so many times before. But things were different now.

The phone rang six times. There was a click as if the call was being transferred to another line. A male voice answered. Not the voice she expected. 'Summerfield here. You have a report?'

Kitty clenched the receiver. She'd no idea what to say.

'McCloud? Is that you?'

Kitty's throat was so tight she could barely speak. 'They know,' she blurted.

There was a shuffle of papers and Summerfield spoke again. 'OK, if you've blown your cover I'm going to explain what we do now. You need to listen very carefully. The team from Station X might have worked out what you've been doing. But you can still be of use to us. We'll bring you home to London.'

It was the use of the word 'team' which made Kitty start to cry.

Brodie Bray was scared.

She held a small, very old book, filled with pictures

and writing. But she couldn't read it.

Brodie Bray was good at reading. Most would say she was exceptional. She read all the time. But she couldn't read this, because the book was in code.

For over two years now, Brodie had been part of a team of children and adults trying to work out how to read MS 408, a book which Level Five of the government's Black Chamber had banned people from even looking at. They'd failed. And now things were getting really serious.

Someone had died.

Tandi Tandari had been Brodie's friend. More than that really, she'd been like an older sister. Brodie didn't have any brothers or sisters. She didn't have a mum and, up until several months ago, she hadn't even known her dad. Now her whole world had got mixed up. And she was scared.

When she'd been very young, her granddad, who'd raised her, had taken her to the local leisure centre. There were two pools. One was called the 'Fun Pool' and it was always full of toddlers thrashing about in armbands, teenagers hitting each other with floats and loud tinny music crackling through the sound system. Next door was the 'Diving Pool'. It was silent. Balanced above the unmoving water was a long, narrow blue board. It went nowhere, just stretched out into the cold, thin air. The board was five metres above the surface of the water. There were silver metal steps to the top. There was no handrail.

Brodie wanted to dive from the board. She wanted to plunge into the deep, dark water and curl her back like a mermaid and then burst through the surface and gasp for air.

But she was scared.

Her granddad stood beside the edge of the water. He reached out, as if he could almost catch her. And he talked to her. All the time, he kept talking. She could even remember what he said. Words of a poem she didn't quite understand. Words about being brave. *'Trust your heart if the seas catch fire; live by love though the stars walk backward.'*

Her toes curled around the lip of the board. Her skin looked so white and the water so far below was almost black with depth. If she could turn back from the end of the board she would. But turning would make her fall, she was sure. She wanted to lower herself down on to the board. Press her body flat against the support and cling to the edge, until someone came. But no one could. When you'd gone that far, there was only one way down. Diving. And her granddad's story said she should trust her heart.

So in that moment of fear, she moved herself

forward through the air. The tipping point came. There was no changing her mind. And as she fell towards the water, any air she had inside her left her mouth in a scream.

The water wrapped around her. She wasn't sure where the surface was. It was dark. So cold it burned. But even in that moment, when the danger was more real than it had ever been on the top of the diving board, she was no longer afraid.

It wasn't the water which was the source of fear. It was making the commitment to dive. It was being alone, launching off and letting go.

Now she was in the secret-breaking Team Veritas, Brodie was no longer alone. She had friends: Hunter and Tusia and Sheldon. And adults like Mr and Mrs Smithies and Ingham and Fabyan to help them. And now she had her dad. Friedman.

But they'd lost Tandi.

And that made Brodie feel like she'd done all those years ago on top of the diving board waiting to dive.

Tandi died in a fire which raged through the grounds of Riverbank Labs and the most terrible thing was, she'd died because they'd been betrayed. They thought Kitty was on their side, but she'd let Suppressors working for the British government know where Team Veritas was. The Suppressors started a fire. Flames took Tandi and destroyed the estate. Only ash remained.

They buried Miss Tandari beside a tree in the grounds. A small wooden cross marked the place. Brodie wanted them to build a large stone monument like the ones they'd seen in Westminster Abbey. This would take time, Fabyan said. Time to do things properly. So for the moment, two pieces of wood tacked together with a rusty nail were all that marked the place where Tandi fell.

Brodie came to the grave each morning and sat with the book and she tried to make sense of the pictures and words and all that had happened.

And she couldn't.

Today though, Brodie wasn't alone at the side of the grave.

'You want some chocolate?' Hunter Jenkins stood above her, shielding his eyes from the sun.

'It's seven thirty in the morning.'

'What? And you think that's too early?' Hunter tried to hide the incredulity from his voice and bit off another square of Hershey bar. 'Never too early for chocolate, BB.' Food was one of Hunter's obsessions. Food and maths. What Hunter could do with numbers was incredible. No less incredible was the amount of food he could eat. Why he wasn't the size of a house

7

was a puzzle she'd been unable to solve! Odd, though, how much taller he'd grown since she'd first met him. How strong he looked now. He was growing into himself was how her granddad explained it.

Hunter sat down beside her and continued to munch. 'You OK?'

'No.' There was no point lying.

'Thinking about Kitty, right?'

Brodie shrugged. 'Trying not to. She let us down. What more's there to say?'

'People do that, B. Sometimes they have reasons.'

'Reasons?'

'I'm not saying that's an excuse.' He raised his hands defensively. 'I'm just saying.'

'Well, don't. Nothing can excuse what she did.' Brodie pulled up a blade of grass. The silver bangle felt warm on her wrist. The bracelet had been Tandi's. It was engraved with glyphs from MS 408, letters she'd never been able to read. 'I wasn't really thinking about Kitty,' Brodie said. 'I was thinking about Tandi. And this.' She gestured to the book in her lap. 'And how much she wanted to read it.'

'Yeah, well. Don't we all?'

'But she gave up so much. A job in the government and time with her family. And it was Tandi who persuaded us to let Kitty join. Remember?'

'I thought you didn't want to talk about her. And if we've learnt nothing else from all of this, it's that people let other people down. Look at the "Cambridge Five". Some of the best code-crackers in the country. Members of the Cambridge Apostles.'

Brodie remembered all their work on the Cambridge Apostles. Finding out about them had been part of cracking some of the codes they'd worked on. Some of the Apostles were part of a secret society trying to keep the knowledge of MS 408 safe. But she wasn't sure why Hunter was talking numbers again – apart from that's what Hunter did, when he wasn't eating. 'Cambridge Five?' she said.

'Spies. Working for the other side. Some of the most clever men in the country and they betrayed those they knew and loved.' He smiled sheepishly. 'But I won't let you down, B. You can be sure of that.'

She twisted the blade of grass and let it fall.

Across in the sooty ruins of the estate, a little boy with the blondest hair and the bluest eyes Brodie had ever seen was playing. Tandi's brother had flown in with the family for the funeral. She watched as he dragged a charred stick across the ground. It made shapes as it moved and dust lifted in clouds. In his other hand he held a wooden statue of an elephant. The Jumbo Rush Elephant had belonged to Tandi.

Her little brother was making it fly.

'Why d'you think Miss Tandari didn't tell us?' Brodie said.

'About Adam, you mean?' said Hunter, finishing the last square of chocolate and looking across at the boy who played in the ruins.

'She just never said, did she?'

'What? About him being white, you mean? Or about him having Down's syndrome?'

'Either,' said Brodie.

'What did you expect her to say? I'm black but my adopted brother isn't? Or, by the way, my brother has special needs. We all have special needs, B.'

'It's just, I was surprised.'

'I guess to her those things weren't worth mentioning. Adam was just Adam.'

'But I don't understand.'

'Why she wouldn't say?'

Brodie was embarrassed. 'No. About Down's syndrome and how it works.'

Hunter leant back on the grass. 'It's a maths thing,' he said confidently. 'All down to numbers. We've got twenty-three pairs of chromosomes in our DNA which makes forty-six, right? Well, Down's syndrome is when a person has an extra chromosome. Number twenty-one sort of doubles up.'

'And that's why Adam is the way he is?'

'There's lots of reasons for why someone is the way they are, B. How he's been brought up, the things he's done.'

'So d'you think he understands what's happened to Tandi?' she said.

'Do *you* understand it?'

Brodie shook her head.

'I know one thing,' said Hunter.

'Go on.'

'He loves this book.' He called over and the boy lifted his head and dropped the stick he held. 'Want to come and chat, Adam?'

The little boy came and sat between them. He gave Brodie the Jumbo Rush Elephant to hold. It was dusted with ash.

'So, mate,' Hunter said. 'You want to look at Tandi's book with us?'

'Tandi's book?'

'Shall we look at the flowers? There are weird flowers, right?'

Adam laughed. 'Look at the islands,' he said.

Brodie knew which page he was talking about. It was her favourite page.

Some of the pages in the manuscript were so large and complicated they folded out of the copy.

The page with the islands was one of these.

Brodie spread the page on her knees.

There were nine islands and they were linked with a sort of causeway. Each island was patterned with blue and lilac ink. Intricate, twisting, repeated patterns like the folds of underwater coral. On one island was a picture of a castle. Tall and elegant, standing proud on the edge of the island.

'Tandi's castle,' said Adam, quietly pressing his little fingers on the page.

'Tandi's castle,' Brodie repeated. The castle of Avalon belonged to all of them. And they wanted so much to find it.

When she'd first joined Team Veritas, her granddad had given Brodie a beautiful locket which used to belong to her mother. Pressed inside was a hand-drawn sketch of the castle. Her mother had spent years trying to make sense of MS 408, and finding the castle was all she'd wanted. Now, all their searching and their puzzle solving had taught them only that the castle was in Avalon. All their research made them believe that the place from stories and legends was actually real. That people had been there. Somehow, since Tandi's death, the belief they'd ever find the castle for themselves had drifted away on the wind like the ash from the fire.

Adam turned the page, folding it awkwardly back into place, and he pointed to the encoded glyphs and patterns scrawled across the manuscript. 'Read it,' he said.

'I can't,' Brodie said.

Adam frowned. His eyes looked paler blue. 'Where's Tandi's castle?' he said.

'We'll find it,' she said.

The way Adam looked at her made Brodie think he really believed her.

'I'm just saying we need to get on with it.' Brodie wasn't in the mood for arguments. The team met in the charred remains of the windmill in the centre of the grounds. It was where Tandi had been working just before she died.

'We should wait a while. Show some respect,' hissed Tusia, who was normally so good at picking up on people's moods and feelings.

Brodie looked around. In the skeletal remains of the windmill it seemed totally clear Tusia might be right. Sheldon was quiet. It was odd for him not to be playing some musical instrument or humming. Brodie hadn't been sure at first he was even there. Friedman was in the corner standing with Sicknote Ingham who was rubbing his chest dramatically, suggesting the ash and soot were troubling his breathing more than anyone else's. Fabyan stood in the shadows, next to Hunter. They looked embarrassed, as if they shouldn't be there. Even Brodie's granddad wasn't meeting her gaze.

'It's just too soon,' said Tusia.

Brodie looked away through the broken ribs of the windmill. In the silence, she almost believed she could still hear the sound of the fire. Even so, she knew they were wrong. The way to keep a memory alive was to strive on. Smithies had said that. 'I don't think it is,' she whispered.

Mrs Smithies stepped forward. Her face was lined. She was concentrating hard, searching for the right words to say. 'Brodie's right,' she said.

Mrs Smithies was the last person Brodie thought would understand. She'd been trapped by the pain of the death of her daughter for years, and yet when Tandi died it was true Mrs Smithies had been the only one who seemed to know what to say. Something Brodie didn't quite understand had happened to her. She'd been set free somehow.

'If we don't find Avalon now,' said Mrs Smithies, 'it makes it all a waste.'

Brodie stepped a little closer. She wanted to show her she knew how brave she was being. How brave they'd all have to be. Mrs Smithies' face flickered into a fragile smile.

'OK,' said Smithies. He looked proud, like he'd been waiting for this moment. As if he'd wanted Brodie and his wife to take the lead. 'If we can agree it's time, then that's what we do.'

Friedman pointed to the blackened husk of the building. 'But all our notes. All the things we'd worked out. It was all here. Along with all the things Tandi had worked out about the Suppressors and just never had the time to tell us.'

Fabyan looked down at the ground. He'd been with Tandi, while the others had been hunting in the Blue Ridge Mountains for the map, but Tandi had never had the time to tell even him the final things she'd discovered about the Suppressors. She'd been excited, he knew. She'd uncovered something big about the people the Suppressors had taken away and held captive. But everything she knew had died with her.

'I have our logbooks,' Brodie said. 'Tandi said we should always be collectors. We can't know what she wanted to tell us, but everything we've talked about I've written down.'

'Everything?' said Hunter. 'Because that conversation about nose hair wasn't really something I wanted recorded for ever.'

Brodie grimaced. 'Everything which was *important*.'

'And we've got the map,' said Tusia. Searching for a map to Avalon was the thing which had brought them to the United States in the first place and it was while they were returning from their treasure hunt that the fire at Riverbank began.

'So we're all on board then?' Smithies asked.

When only a muffled cough from Sicknote's

direction broke the silence, Brodie guessed that was a yes.

'OK,' Smithies said, balancing his glasses on his forehead. 'Let's recap everything we know.'

In the house, minutes later, in one of the undamaged rooms where they kept their things, Tusia cleared a space on a rickety table. Then she took the logbook and flicked through the pages. 'MS 408's the centre of everything. All the codes we've solved help us make sense of Voynich's coded manuscript.'

'Codes left behind by Knights of Neustria,' added Hunter, 'named after the very first three Knights of Neustria: Sir Bedivere and his children, Amren and Eneuvac.'

'And Sir Bedivere was a knight of King Arthur, and his job, when the king was dying, was to return the sword Excalibur to the waters of a lake so it could be returned to Avalon,' said Tusia. 'And so we worked out MS 408 was about Avalon and everything makes us think the place really exists.'

'And that people had been there,' added Hunter, always enjoying the opportunity to correct Tusia.

'Yeah, OK. I was getting to that. We think Renata, who was buried in the tomb at Shugborough, had been there, and that's why we ended up over here in

# Everything we know…

MS408

The Knights of Neustria → Sir Bedivere
→ Amren
→ Eneuvac

So…

MS408 = about AVALON

which really exists! → we think…

went to Avalon?

Shugborough

Treasure → taken from Avalon
taken by Suppressors!

# The Suppressors

don't want us to prove Avalon exists

this scared Helen Weaver too!

PIGAFETTA

*Hans of Aachen + Martin de Judicibus

left in
code in library
of Congress *

Nice chicken
again, B!

drew
map

America tracking down the treasure we thought had been taken from Avalon.'

'Which has now been taken from us by the Suppressors,' said Sicknote.

'Yes, well, we knew it was a dangerous game we were in,' said Smithies. 'We always knew the Suppressors wanted us to leave MS 408 alone. Reading it would be one thing. But finding the actual location of Avalon would just be too much for them. We know they don't want us to prove there's a place where people can live well together . . . where everything is fair. They're not in the business of fairness.'

'And the idea's scared other people too,' added Sicknote. 'Remember Elgar's girlfriend, Helen Weaver? She ran away to New Zealand when he told her the secret about Avalon existing. Knowing that a place which is talked about in myth actually really exists could frighten people.'

'Or make them crazy to go there themselves looking for treasure,' said Friedman.

'That's what the Suppressors wanted in the end, wasn't it? Apart from stopping us doing our research, they wanted the treasure in the Blue Mountains for themselves.'

'But they didn't get everything, did they?' added Fabyan.

Brodie reached up to her locket. 'No. We found a sword with the name Pigafetta engraved on it but we mustn't forget that my locket and the ring Fabyan tracked down were important too.'

Fabyan's grin broadened.

'So let's check the names we found on the locket and the ring,' said Sheldon.

Tusia read from the logbook. 'Hans of Aachen and Martin de Judicibus.'

'More Knights of Neustria,' said Sheldon. 'One for the griffin, one for the tree and one for the phoenix. The three emblems of the Knights.'

Tusia looked again at the logbook. 'Hans of Aachen was the link with the book called the *Morte d'Arthur*, remember. The book which was saved from burning and helped us to tighten the link with King Arthur.'

'And Martin de Judicibus drew the map,' added Hunter, reading over her shoulder. 'We've no idea what this Pigafetta guy did but we know it must be important because his name was left in code in the Library of Congress.'

'We've got Hans and Martin and Pigafetta. And we know they're Knights of Neustria. That's enough for now.'

Hunter pulled a face. 'Not like you to leave out all the stuff to do with libraries, B.'

'I know. I know. But if you get me thinking about the Library of Congress and the stories we saw painted on the walls there about Prometheus stealing the fire, then my mind will just race away.'

'Hans, Martin, Pigafetta,' Smithies said matter-of-factly. 'Knights of Neustria. And a map to Avalon. Let's stick with that.'

Brodie rubbed her head. It didn't stop the whole thing feeling like a knotted ball of string in her mind and she still couldn't find the end.

'All these pieces put together,' Smithies said, 'suggests Avalon exists.'

'So are we ready then?' Friedman said. 'To look at the map and find Avalon?'

'It's come down to this?' Kerrith Vernan stood at the end of the table, leaning her weight on her hands so that her face was just centimetres away from the teenage girl who sat in front of her.

Kitty McCloud was sobbing.

'They worked out you were no friend of theirs and you've come crawling back to England.'

'Everything went wrong,' Kitty spluttered.

Kerrith stood up straight. She shot a glance towards the corner of the room. Summerfield was scribbling on a clipboard. He'd hoped to deal with the return of an agent from the field himself but Kerrith had made things very clear. It was her job to make sure Miss McCloud understood how things would work now. The fact that Kitty *owed* the Black Chamber had to be made clear to her. It was key she knew she should do all that was asked of her. Kerrith understood that Kitty's mental well-being depended on it.

'If you want to keep your freedom, Miss McCloud,' Kerrith said, 'you are to be stationed at my home from now on. You are to report to me at all times. About everything. Understood?' She leant forward again and her face was so close to Kitty's that she could see the whites of her eyes. 'There are some things I need to talk through with you.'

Summerfield stopped writing on the clipboard. Kerrith was reassured that he now knew she had everything under control. Her plan was only just taking shape, but the McCloud girl had nowhere left to run. And that made her useful.

The Martin de Judicibus map was the next step in the puzzle. And it was time they looked properly.

Tusia took the yellowed scroll and let it unroll. She weighted each corner down and Adam, who'd been playing in the grounds until he saw them returning from the windmill, nosed to the front.

The image was intricate and detailed and yet great spaces were blank and unmarked. Dark shadowing reached the edges but near the centre there was a ring of yellow around a speckled blue background. To Brodie it looked like a circle of flame. Perhaps the map wasn't quite finished, locations not yet explored.

Adam's chin was resting on the table. He pointed to the furthest corner. 'Islands,' he said.

Brodie peered closer.

She could feel Hunter's breath on her shoulder. He was counting. 'Nine,' he said. 'There's nine islands on the corner of the map just like there are nine islands in MS 408.'

The doctor stood at the end of the bed. He held a clipboard and flicked through the notes clamped to it with the sort of detachment used by bored people, sitting in dentists' waiting rooms, forced to resort to looking through out-of-date fishing magazines.

'When was he admitted?'

'Two weeks ago.' The answering nurse had no need to refer to notes. She knew the patient's history off by heart.

'And the reason for his admission?'

'Initially we thought he'd just collapsed in a bar. He was having problems breathing. Looked like smoke inhalation for a while.'

'And now?'

'We're sure he's suffering from some sort of encephalitis.'

'So this man has a sleeping sickness,' said the doctor. 'And you think it's been brought on by what exactly?'

The nurse moved closer to the bed. She turned the patient's head and showed a small, raised red lump on the back of his neck. 'Mosquito bite.'

The doctor flicked the pages of his notes again, this time more keenly.

'He was an emergency admission,' the nurse went on. 'We'd barely started going through his medical history before he could no longer understand what we were asking, so it was difficult to establish where in the world he'd been and where he could have picked up the disease from. But he reacted aggressively to the sight of needles and it's my opinion he hadn't had any vaccinations to prevent disease.'

'And there's been no contact with relatives or friends?' the doctor asked.

'Nothing. No one's been near. Not even sure anyone close to him would know he'd been admitted.'

'But he must have had identification. Something that connects him to someone else or a place.'

'I don't think he wanted anyone to know who he was. Secrecy must have been important to him.'

'So you found nothing that could help us work out who he was?'

'Only these.' She held out her hand. Two silver cuff links rocked back and forth.

The doctor was intrigued. He took one and held it up to the light. 'So the fire theme's not a new one,' he said, peering at the etching on the cuff link. 'Weird.'

'He certainly has a thing about fire,' said the nurse. 'In the moments before he became silent, he was obviously hallucinating. Kept rambling on about flames and destruction.'

The doctor hung the clipboard on the end of the bed. 'My most likely guess is he's got West Nile fever,' he said. 'Explains the coma now and the confusion earlier. I'm of the opinion you're right, Nurse Evans. The tiny mosquito *is* the bringer of this man's problems. I fear we may be too late.'

The nurse lowered her head. Even if the patient couldn't hear she felt awkward discussing such things so close to the end of his bed. 'You think he'll die?'

The doctor took a deep breath and began to walk down the ward. 'I think the man's system has been defeated by something so small and tiny that we as humans hardly give it any thought. Yes, I think this man will die. And I don't think it will be long before he does.' He didn't even glance over his shoulder at the nurse, who was still loitering by the bed. 'The best we can do is make him comfortable.' Then he reached down to pick up the clipboard from the end of the next bed in line.

# The Mark of
# Lux et Veritas

'I just don't understand why you think this is safe?' said Sicknote as their taxi pulled to a halt.

'And you think staying back at Riverbank was safer?' said Smithies, paying the driver and stepping back as the car pulled away. 'We've got to face facts now, Oscar. And the facts are these. All the while MS 408 was a banned document, we avoided looking at the real thing. We made do with copies. Two weeks ago, the rules to this game changed. The Suppressors are stopping at nothing. Neither must we.' Brodie huddled closer to be sure she didn't miss a word. 'Before we go any further we must have a look at the actual Voynich Manuscript. Who knows what little details we're missing which might make the whole thing click into place.' Smithies steered the group towards the signs for the Hewitt University Quadrangle. 'Besides. We're in America with an American billionaire. Money, as they say, talks, and Fabyan has arranged us a private viewing.'

They'd discussed coming to Yale University before. Brodie could hardly believe they were actually here. Since the very first day at Station X, when she'd received her copy of MS 408 in a small wooden trunk, she'd thought of the document as the real thing. It was odd to think that all the while the real, tiny leather-bound document had actually been locked up here.

All around her, students hurried past. There were eateries and bookshops lining either side of the street and outside one particularly large café there was a group of tables where customers sat playing chess. 'He needs to move white knight to c6,' Tusia said, 'otherwise his king's vulnerable.'

No one answered her. Puzzles caused by shape and space consumed Tusia. With Brodie, it was all about the story. And the home of the story of MS 408 was the Beinecke Rare Book and Manuscript Library. Brodie felt excited, like it was the night before her birthday.

'Now, promise me,' said Sheldon, hurrying from his own taxi to walk beside her, 'that you won't have one of your turns when we go inside.'

'My turns?'

'Like you did in New York and then in the Library of Congress. It's just a library.'

She was going to argue but, like asking Tusia not to mention chess moves, she knew there was little point.

'You're fine, B,' said Hunter. 'It's cool you get excited. I like that.'

Brodie smiled smugly at Sheldon. If she was excited when she saw the library then he'd just have to get over it. It was 'her thing' and . . .

They turned the corner. Friedman stopped. The group stumbled to a halt behind him.

Brodie felt like she'd been punched very hard in the stomach. 'Is that it?'

The building in front of them looked like a large, grey concrete box. It was a huge cuboid that was floating somehow, its sides covered in smaller squares which looked like they'd been creased and folded round the edges.

'Fifteen by five. Nice,' said Hunter.

Brodie stared at him, hoping that whatever the explanation was for what he'd said, it would make her feel better.

'The squares along the side. They're arranged fifteen along and five up. It's nice.'

'It's awful, that's what it is,' groaned Brodie, scanning the beautiful old buildings surrounding the library. 'Where are the windows, for a start?'

'Ahh,' said Granddad, moving to stand beside her. 'I remember reading about this when the thing was built. No windows to stop the books getting light damaged or aged. I think they wanted to use onyx originally, but they didn't have enough. So they went for slabs of marble instead. They have to control light and humidity.'

'But—'

Smithies didn't wait for her to be reassured. 'I think you'll find you understand a little more about their decision when you get inside. Everything isn't always what it seems.'

They made their way towards the revolving doorway, with Brodie trying hard not to sulk.

'Hey,' said Sheldon, trying desperately to lift her mood and make up for earlier. 'You'll like this though. Look.' He directed her towards a plaque positioned on the wall which explained about the dedication of the library. '*It is a symbol of devotion and loyalty between three brothers,*' he read, '*built to serve as a source of learning and inspiration for all who enter.* You like that bit, surely.'

Brodie wasn't sure how anyone could be

inspired inside a concrete box.

'Knights of Neustria tend to come in threes, B,' added Hunter hopefully, and suddenly Sheldon looked a little awkward.

Brodie didn't say anything. She stepped into the revolving door and the world spun round.

And as the world turned she understood. Something magical happened to the light once you stepped inside. What she'd supposed were solid concrete blocks all along the side of the building were in fact squares of translucent marble. Light seeped through the surface, finding entry through veins in the stone. In that moment, Brodie was back lying on her bed, holding up a puzzle card in the air, and the light found its way through the holes to give her answers to the code that brought her to the start of this whole adventure. Suddenly she felt warm, as if the light was bathing her.

'Guess now you get it,' said Smithies, tapping her gently on the arm. 'Things are not always what they seem.'

In the centre of the building, growing like a tree, was a tower of books encased in glass. Two stairways curled up on either side to the mezzanine level above.

'We going up?' asked Tusia, striding forward.

Fabyan raised his hand. 'I've agreed to meet Mr

Watson down in the Reading Room,' he said, turning towards a lower staircase. 'But first there's the matter of security.'

The woman at the reception desk seemed particularly amused by the photograph in Hunter's passport. 'I was hungry,' he said, frowning sulkily at the mugshot. 'The camera caught me at a bad time.'

Tusia muttered something which Brodie guessed was rude.

'We should hurry. We don't want to be late,' said Fabyan, leading the way to the stairs down to the basement.

On the lower level of the building was a long corridor. Fabyan glanced at his notes and then the numbers on the doors. The room they wanted was near the end. A small room arranged with tables and chairs. A regular reading room, but it was the far wall which shocked Brodie. This time the whole wall was window, a bank of glass, floor to ceiling. It was darkened, so the view outside was sepia coloured. And what she could see outside seemed rather strange.

'It's called a garden,' Fabyan said. 'Mr Watson explained.'

'Well, that's weird,' said Sheldon, pressing his nose against the glass. 'Not like any garden I've seen.'

Tusia hurried to join him.

# Garden at the Beinecke Rare Book + Manuscript Library

picture of Arcadia + Mad Jack Fuller's tomb!

Coleridge + Francis Bacon rings

EARTH

SUN

pyramid

ring

cube

CHANCE

the garden links with the knights' codes!

The garden was made of concrete. A flat surface had been marked with lines and on top of the surface were three things. A pyramid. A ring. And a cube balancing on one of its corners.

'Bonkers,' said Hunter.

'We prefer to use the word "art".' A tall man, in a tight-fitting suit, had entered the room. His hair was grey and wiry and on the end of his nose a pair of glasses was so precariously balanced Brodie was sure any moment soon they'd slip to the floor. His accent was soft and smooth; any harsh American twang had been trained away after hours of speaking in hushed tones.

'Mr Watson,' beamed Fabyan, striding forward, his hand outstretched.

The visitor grimaced and raised his arms, displaying crisp white gloves on each hand. 'I come prepared,' he said. 'The merest handshake risks contamination of the documents.'

Fabyan looked abashed. 'For sure. For sure.' He lowered his arm apologetically. 'We were just saying how wonderful the garden was.'

'Yes. Well, it's what the garden symbolises that's important,' he said through breathy tones.

'And that is?' asked Friedman.

Mr Watson drew closer to the window. 'The

pyramid: the earth itself, and all the wonderful geometry it contains. The ring: the sun, of course. That one's obvious. And the cube there, balanced as it is on one tiny corner, represents chance. A most remarkable work.'

What Brodie thought was remarkable was how tightly the garden tied in with the codes of the Knights of Neustria. The rings of Coleridge and Francis Bacon which contained the codes, and the pyramid that had been on the picture of Arcadia and on the tomb of Mad Jack Fuller.

But the cube meant nothing.

Not yet, anyway.


'So, are you ready?'

Brodie turned from the window. Mr Watson had reappeared in the doorway of the Reading Room and this time he held two boxes. The door clicked shut behind him.

Mr Watson put the boxes on the table and lifted the lid of the first. 'Correspondence,' he said. 'Letters connected to the manuscript.'

Brodie waited for him to explain.

He took several sheets of paper from the box. 'These are letters from Anne Nills. She was the executor of Ethel Voynich's will. Voynich himself had high hopes for the document and believed it would make him a fortune. When he died, the manuscript passed first to his wife and then to Ms Nills. And then, of course, it made its way here to be catalogued in the general collection as MS 408.'

He took another stack of letters. 'These are from Theodore Peterson. Mainly about the age of the document. It's believed by most that the manuscript is about five hundred years old.' He lifted another sheet of paper. 'And this one's my personal favourite. In Latin, of course. It's from Johannes Marcus Marci of Cronland when he presented the manuscript to Athanasius Kircher in Rome. Kircher was a master code-cracker. But the master failed with this one. Still, the letter's good. Gives us a bit of history about the manuscript. Explains the manuscript was once owned by the Emperor Rudolph.'

'Who was he?' asked Hunter.

'He was around at the same time as your English Queen Elizabeth the First.'

Brodie racked her brains. Elizabeth lived in the late fifteen hundreds. The same time as Francis Bacon and his dad and Sir Thomas Malory, some of the first few Knights of Neustria. That would have made Rudolph one of the first owners of the manuscript.

'Rudolph was a collector of oddities,' Mr Watson

# History of MS 408

Letters from Anne Nills → executor of Ethel Voynich's will

Letters from Theodore Peterson

approx. 500 years old?

from Johannes Marcus Marci of Cronland

gave MS 408 to Athanasius Kircher - master code cracker

owned by Emperor Rudolph → ♥ the arts + stories

a recluse

childhood in Spain

Covadonga!

'Cabinet of Curiosities'

Prague Castle → <u>MS408</u> → sold

→ Prof. Newbold    Was he mad?

↳ glyphs = microscopic writing

continued, 'which is why I guess this manuscript found its way to him. He was fascinated by the arts and stories of worlds beyond ours.'

Brodie felt her skin prickle and she could see Mr Watson was excited too.

'Rudolph was a recluse much of his life, although I believe his childhood in Spain was a happy one.'

Spain. Brodie was making connections in her mind with the Spanish sailing ship *Covadonga*.

'He kept at Prague Castle something called a "Cabinet of Curiosities". It was so large, he built a whole new wing of the castle to store his collection. And MS 408 was housed there. But,' Mr Watson screwed up his nose as if he'd smelt something unpleasant, 'those who came after Rudolph didn't think much of his strange collection and so the pieces were sold on and dispersed. MS 408 slipped out of the history books for a while until Voynich's happy find.'

Mr Watson turned once more to the box. The final wodge of letters he lifted out were thicker. 'These are just the ramblings of one mad man to another who wanted so much to own a manuscript which could change the world.'

'By that you mean . . . ?' cut in Sicknote.

'Voynich was the ultimate collector,' he said. There was a sense of admiration in his voice. 'He collected for himself, not for the authorities or his country. But these letters are from the ultimate collector to the ultimate delusionary. Professor Newbold.'

'Heard of him,' whispered Hunter. 'And I think Watson might be right about the Newbold-being-mad thing.'

Mr Watson ploughed on. 'Newbold had the crazy idea that each of the glyphs in the manuscript was actually broken into several separate parts and it was each of these pieces of microscopic writing which really hid the message of the manuscript.'

'And you think he was wrong?' asked Tusia.

'I *know* he was wrong. And so did everybody who turned up to hear his lecture on the decipherment. Still, loads of people have had a go at making sense of this thing. Can't blame a man for trying.'

'Yes,' said Friedman, moving impatiently from foot to foot. 'About that. Any chance of us being able to see the actual thing any time soon?'

Mr Watson's gaze was withering. He replaced the letters in the box marked 'B' and opened the other box. Inside was a small parcel wrapped in folds of fabric. 'MS 408,' he said without ceremony. 'I believe it was this you've come all the way to see.'

Brodie wasn't sure what she expected. It wasn't this.

The front cover was tatty. Brown scratched leather

pulled unevenly across yellow leaves which stuck out at the edges. It had no embossing. No golden writing meticulously placed across the middle. And it was small. Smaller than she'd imagined.

Mr Watson put the book down on a slab of foam which looked to Brodie too modern to hold something so old. Then, with gloved hands, he began to turn the pages. The air crackled.

Inside the front cover was a small paper label with the stamp of the university. Brodie peered in closer to see.

The motto of Yale University was written across the label. She said the words inside her head. '*Lux et Veritas*'.

'Lux? What does that mean?' asked Tusia.

Mr Watson looked up. He looked confused. 'You know what Veritas means then, I take it?'

'Truth,' said Hunter. 'We get that. It's the Lux bit we don't know.'

'Light,' said Mr Watson. The pages crackled as he turned them. '"Light and truth" is the motto of Yale University.'

And it was then that any disappointment Brodie felt just ebbed away.

As she looked down at the very first page of MS 408 she knew without question that she was looking at the most incredible manuscript in the world.

* * *

The garden outside the Reading Room was growing dark by the time Brodie and the others reached the last page of the manuscript. With every turn of paper, Brodie had fallen deeper.

She loved books. What she felt for the manuscript, though, was something stronger. A feeling she didn't really understand. She wondered if it was what Sheldon felt when he listened to music. A sense that the world outside could stop, or change, or maybe even melt away, and it wouldn't matter.

Having the copies of the manuscript had been wonderful. Photos of the pages had kept her awake at night, puzzling and wondering. But the real thing, although it was identical, was different. She ached to know what it said.

Knowing that at any moment Mr Watson was going to rewrap the manuscript in linen and take it from them, Brodie blurted out, 'Page eighty-six. Can we see it again?'

Mr Watson straightened the foam bedding in front of him and lifted the folded page from the manuscript so it extended. And there it was. The picture of the nine islands inked in blue and lilac. And the castle.

Could a ship really have travelled to those islands? Could that be Avalon?

Outside in the garden, a tiny bird landed on the corner of the sculpted cube.

'It's odd, don't you think,' said Sheldon, 'that we've come halfway round the world to see this?'

'I don't think you'll find the distance between Bletchley and New Haven, Connecticut is actually equal to halfway around the world,' Tusia corrected quietly.

'Furthest I've ever been,' said Sheldon.

'Yes, well. Me too, really, but even in the time of Rudolph and Queen Elizabeth the First some people had completed circumnavigation.'

It was obvious Sheldon didn't know what this word meant.

'Circumnavigation,' Tusia repeated. 'It means all the way around the world.'

Mr Watson looked up. 'If you're interested in circumnavigation, we've got a document here in the library written by one of the very first people in the world to complete that journey.'

'That's very kind,' said Mr Smithies. 'But our interest is purely in MS 408.'

'Suit yourself,' said Mr Watson. 'Some visitors find looking at documents which can actually be read far more beneficial than looking at things which are totally impossible to make sense of.' He refolded page

86. 'And I personally find the writing of Antonio Pigafetta absolutely fascinating.'

The bird in the garden flew away from the corner of the cube.

'Antonio who?' said Brodie softly.

'Antonio Pigafetta,' said Mr Watson. 'Why?'

The door opened.

A woman, short and petite, entered the room.

She gestured to Mr Watson, who stepped away from the document table and leant forward to be able to hear her. It was impossible to make out what she said. Her whisper was so low and her accent so pronounced, the words were meaningless. Mr Watson understood. When he turned to look at them, his face had greyed and his cheeks were pinched.

He bundled MS 408 into its wrapping and put it back in the box. 'I'm afraid I have matters to attend to. Other people to see and, despite your most generous donation to the work of the library, Mr Fabyan, I'm afraid my time availability is at an end.'

'What?'

'I have to go.'

'But the manuscript. We needed longer. And Pigafetta. You told us about Pigafetta.'

'MS 408 must be returned. It's kept in controlled

temperature and humidity conditions. It has already been out of safety for long enough.' He struggled to place the lid securely on the box. 'It's been made perfectly clear to me by my superiors that it's time for our little consultation to come to an end. Now, if you would be so kind, those in charge of the library would be most grateful if you could leave.'

'Mr Watson, please. The Pigafetta document. You mentioned something about—'

Mr Watson obviously had no intention of being delayed.

Fabyan stepped to block the doorway, which had shut firmly behind the library worker who'd hurried from the room after delivering her message. 'Mr Watson, if you would just—'

'I'm afraid you don't understand!' The curator clutched the boxes close to his chest, his gloved hands digging tight into the cardboard. 'I really have to go. The library shows MS 408 to no one, but your donation seemed so generous, so fitting. But I'm afraid the situation's changed. The decision to share with you has been withdrawn. You need to leave Yale. And quickly.'

Brodie looked out of the window. Two shadowed figures in smart grey suits were standing at the edge of the garden.

Fabyan squared his shoulders. The exit was firmly barred. 'Mr Watson, we've come a long way. Not all the way round the world, I'll grant you. Not even halfway round, as my friend Tusia was so keen to point out. But we've come, without doubt, a very long distance. You could say it's taken over two years of travelling for us to get here. And if you think, after giving us such a fascinating glimmer of information, you can simply pack up your boxes and disappear then you're very much mistaken. America is in charge of the archives here.' He too glanced over at the window and saw the two men waiting in the shadows. Brodie knew what he thought. They'd been followed. Suppressors must have found out they were here. But this didn't seem to weaken Fabyan's resolve. 'Whatever you've been told, surely British authorities have no jurisdiction over who sees what in the collections here.'

Brodie was reminded of the way Fabyan had spoken the very first time she'd seen him. Then, he'd been taking on the British government face to face, but it was true to say, he was absolutely no less determined today.

'You don't understand,' said Mr Watson. 'To spend any more time with you is, I now realise, more than my job's worth.'

Fabyan was not a billionaire for nothing. He and

his father and his grandfather before him had learnt the value of persistence and, along the way, the power of persuasion behind the dollar or the pound. 'Take another job,' Fabyan said calmly.

Mr Watson was angry now. 'Don't be ridiculous. *This* is my job. *This* is what I do. Why would I want to leave?'

'Maybe because you're sick of watching others have the leisure to be able to collect and research things for themselves. Maybe because what you really want is to begin to put together your own collection of curiosities. Your own cabinet of collectables where no one can tell you who is, or isn't, allowed to see what.'

Something was changing in Mr Watson's face. Fabyan had struck a nerve and, knowing he had, he played with the curator, like a fish on a line.

'Imagine having the funds to start your own collection. To travel the world like Voynich did and build your own special kingdom of curiosities, owned not by the state, or the public. But by you.'

'I must go.'

'What, and walk away from this once-in-a-lifetime opportunity?'

'What opportunity?'

Fabyan took out a small notebook from his pocket and a pen. He licked the nib of the pen and began to write. 'How about an opportunity this big?' He tore the page from the pad and balanced it on the top of the boxes Mr Watson still clung to.

'That much money? For me?' He hesitated. 'For doing what?'

Fabyan grinned and reeled him in. 'For ignoring the instructions you've obviously just received from the authorities and telling us all about Pigafetta and the document you mentioned.'

3

# Two Sides to Every Story

The Chairman didn't like the Director's office. It was too small. Nothing compared to the palatial suite he enjoyed on the penthouse floor. Shame really, the Director had never got to see that floor of the Chamber.

The Chairman reached into his inside pocket. It was a shame about a lot of things.

He flicked the photograph backwards and forwards. The black and white image seemed so aged now in a world where photos were full colour and most often filled the whole screen on a PC. The printed image from the developer's wallet that you waited so long to collect was a thing of a past he'd spent his whole adult life trying to overcome. He ran his hand across the matt surface of the photo and let his finger hover a moment over the faces smiling out at him. Were they laughing at him then? he wondered. Were they aware how much he longed to be part of what they did? He sniffed and put the photograph away. Then, he had been on the wrong side of the lens. That wasn't true now. If there were still sides, and he knew for certain there were, he was on the right side now.

The knock at the door broke the silence.

When the door swung open, two women stood on the threshold. One young, barely even out of her teens, if at all. The other older, more weathered by life, although it was clear that up until recently she'd been doing her best to keep the weathering at bay.

The Chairman leant back in his chair. 'Welcome, welcome. Come on in.'

The older woman led the way but she looked confused. 'I was expecting the Director.'

'Things change,' said the Chairman. 'I'm afraid the Director is,' he hesitated, enjoying his private joke, 'otherwise engaged. But we shall get to that all in good time. Have a seat, Miss Vernan, Miss McCloud. Please, make yourselves comfortable.'

It was evident by the look on the younger woman's face at least, that she was far from comfortable.

He tried to lighten the mood. 'I'm in charge here. You're quite safe.'

This did little to relax either visitor.

The Chairman stood up. 'Don't be nervous. Here.' He gestured to the side of the room where a display of various artefacts and treasures had been arranged. 'Surely feasting your eyes on such discoveries will improve your mood.' He enjoyed the use of the word 'discoveries'. It could hardly be said the hoards of treasure brought from the Blue Ridge Mountains were really just 'discovered'. That term suggested the objects had been honestly stumbled upon. The memory of how the goods had been seized before the arrival of the team from Station X still had the power to excite him. Revenge, if slow, was still worth the wait.

He turned from the display and looked back at the waiting women. Neither seemed too delighted by what they saw. This irritated him. He walked back to his chair. 'Miss McCloud,' he began, turning to look at the younger woman. 'Your work for the Chamber is greatly appreciated. The way you wormed your way into the confidence of the team from Station X was really exemplary. First-class betrayal,' he said, although these words didn't seem to have the effect he was hoping for and the younger woman lowered her head.

The Chairman turned to the older visitor. The real reason for the meeting. 'I'm glad you're feeling better,

Miss Vernan,' he said. 'One of the last conversations I had with the Director was about his concerns for your health. It was a shame you weren't able to be with him in Illinois. Still. No matter. The task was completed to our satisfaction, and unless my eyes deceive me you are quite well once more, if still a little peaky.'

Kerrith Vernan's face flashed an awkward smile which looked a little like a grimace.

'However,' said the Chairman, cutting to the chase. 'You are probably wondering why I've called you here.'

Neither woman responded.

'Seems illness had another victim,' explained the Chairman. 'And one, I'm afraid, who was not able to fight off sickness as well as you.' He dragged out the silence for dramatic effect. 'Word has reached us, the Director didn't make it back from Illinois. We've got to be careful, of course, about the connections with "operatives" overseas. This is a secret organisation after all. But it would seem the Director was gravely unwell.' His use of words amused him. 'What I'm trying to say is, he died.'

The older woman, at least, looked visibly shocked, although the younger woman showed no reaction.

'Bad news, I'm sure,' went on the Chairman. 'But not for you, Miss Vernan.'

It looked a little as if Miss Vernan might, at any

moment, leave the room to go and be sick. Didn't she have any idea what the news of the death of the Director meant to the Chamber? To her in particular?

'Level Five is, I'm afraid, without a captain, Miss Vernan. With such extensive work on our most pressing case, those in the department, and in fact those in positions of power in the Tyrannos Group, have only one name in mind for the Director's successor.' He opened his arms and leant forward. 'You.'

The older woman's colour drained completely.

'The Chamber needs a new Director. It should be you. The Director's office,' he widened his arms even further, 'control of the treasure and, indeed, responsibility for bringing down all those who work at Station X belongs now to you, Miss Vernan.'

Two pink spots were blooming on the woman's cheeks. The Chairman was relieved. At least she was finally understanding the situation and the implications it had for her.

'I have to say, we're beginning to lose patience,' he added. 'Those at the top of Tyrannos have waited as long as they are prepared to wait. The Director was slow in his decision-making, too cautious in his attempts to reel Smithies and the others in. We've got to up the stakes now, Miss Vernan, and that responsibility will rest with you.' He tapped the table.

'You won't be alone in your task though,' he continued. 'Miss McCloud here has demonstrated a remarkable talent for deception and disloyalty. She will make a reliable support for you as you tackle the next stage of the operation. And I have decided, also, to become more fully involved myself in the operation.'

Miss Vernan nodded. The pink circles on her cheek were scarlet now. Not the reaction he'd expected, if he was honest, but people were complicated. The paperwork suggested there really was no one better for the job than Kerrith Vernan. And he would be watching closely to see.

Kerrith closed the office door and stood for a moment with her back against it. She held a sheaf of classified documents. The Chairman had insisted she make a start right away. Tyrannos, and their influence on suppression, needed to be understood. She needed to be totally up to date if she was going to be Director.

Even in her wildest dreams, she'd never hoped for such promotion so quickly. The title was really all she'd ever hoped for. And now it was hers.

'He's not coming.' Brodie remembered saying something similar months before as she waited on the bridge across the river, back home in England.

Then, the adventure hadn't even really begun. Now, they were so caught up in the dangers of searching for answers, that moment on the bridge seemed like it belonged to someone else's memory. But she remembered the wait. And the belief no one would come.

'He'll be here.' Granddad's faith was unwavering. It had been so, on the bridge. 'We'll give him till eleven.'

Meeting in the Book Trader Cafe had been Mr Watson's idea. He'd made it clear, meeting in the Beinecke was totally out of the question now. The café would be safe, he said. People sat and chatted there for hours, swapping and trading books, hidden behind the shelves which filled the space. No one would bother them. He was sure.

He was also late. And this bothered Brodie.

'Try and relax, B,' said Hunter, noticing her glance again at both her wristwatches. 'Eat some sandwich.'

All the food at the Book Trader Cafe had literary names. Hunter was munching his way through his second serving of a particularly large sandwich named 'Tale of two turkeys'.

'I don't know how you can eat at a time like this,' she said. Hunter frowned and a dollop of relish fell on his plate.

When the door of the café opened, everyone looked up.

Mr Watson was dressed head to toe in black, a striped grey scarf muffling his face. 'Oh, very subtle,' moaned Sheldon.

The curator nodded at the counter staff, walked through the shop and joined the team in a back booth Mr Smithies had chosen because it seemed most discreet.

'You kept us waiting,' said Fabyan in an obvious attempt to remind Watson he'd put a very high price on this meeting. The curator's jaw tightened. It was enough to remind them that no amount of money would make Fabyan the one with the power. It was the curator's knowledge they needed.

Squeezing on to the bench seat beside Friedman, the curator unravelled his scarf. 'I'll have coffee,' he said. 'Black. No sugar.'

When everyone was settled and the drink delivered, Mr Watson cleared his throat. 'You want to know about Pigafetta?' he said, and he took from a briefcase several books and put them on the table. 'Well, ask away.'

'Who was he?' said Sicknote.

'An ancient mariner,' laughed Watson, flicking open the first book on the table.

Brodie opened her logbook and began to write. Ancient mariner. The title of a poem by Coleridge. The very poem she'd learnt off by heart at school and they'd used to help them find the hidden ring in the River Wye in Chepstow. Hunter glanced across the table. She wondered if he was remembering the surging river and how they'd nearly drowned. Ancient mariner. Pigafetta. She wrote it down.

'Of course,' went on Watson, 'most people believe Coleridge drew inspiration for his poem about the mariner from Captain Cook's journeys in the 1700s but Pigafetta was a mariner too. His story begins much earlier. It's no less exciting than Cook's.' He took a mouthful of coffee, cracked his knuckles and began to explain.

'Pigafetta was born in Vicenza in about 1491, although there's debate about the date. He was a learned man. A man of books. And he asked to accompany the Portuguese Captain Ferdinand Magellan and his Spanish crew on their expedition to the Spice Islands. Of a crew of two hundred and forty, who set out in 1519, he was one of only eighteen to return.'

'What happened to the others?' asked Tusia.

'Died,' said Watson.

'Not the best survival rate,' said Hunter. 'Two

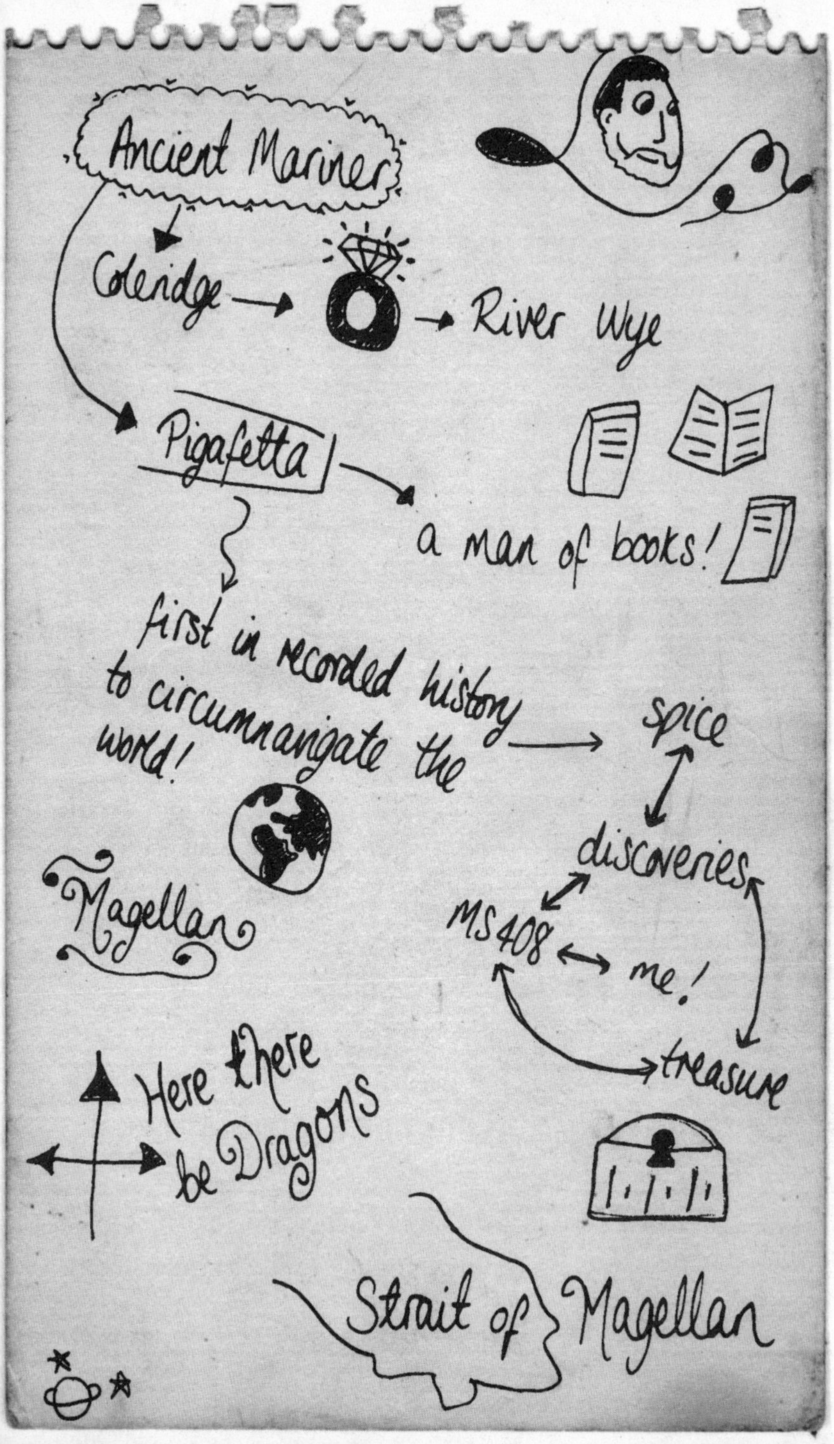

Ancient Mariner
Coleridge
River Wye
Pigafetta
a man of books!
first in recorded history to circumnavigate the world!
spice
discoveries
MS 408
me!
treasure
Magellan
Here there be Dragons
Strait of Magellan

hundred and twenty-two deaths. Can't really go down as a successful trip.'

'Ahh. You're wrong there. If we count success by survival rate, then no, it was not a good trip. But if we count success by achievement, it was one of the most successful trips ever taken by man, or woman, any time in history.'

Brodie and the others made it clear they needed convincing.

'Pigafetta and the other seventeen men were the very first humans in recorded history to complete a circumnavigation of the globe.'

'They were the first to travel all the way round it?' confirmed Tusia.

'The purpose of their journey was to collect spice,' went on Watson.

'What, smelly stuff to put in food?' said Hunter, wiping his now empty plate with the heel of his thumb and licking the crumbs.

'Nutmeg and cloves were of great value then,' said Watson, with a slight look of revulsion on his face. 'The race for spice was like the oil race now and a ship full of spice was treasure unimagined to people living then.'

'And knowing there was a really good chance they'd die if they went looking for it,' said Sicknote, 'men

60

willingly signed up to join the crew, did they?'

'Exploration and discovery of new things,' said Watson. 'Isn't that what drives us? The thought of reaching unreachable places one of the most exciting spurs of the human spirit?'

Brodie smiled to herself. Little did he know about their drive to find undiscovered places.

'It's that drive which makes people climb mountains and travel into space, isn't it?' Watson went on. 'Those two hundred and forty knew the risk, but for the rewards they'd receive and the places they'd see, it was a risk they were willing to take.'

Brodie twisted the pen. What she felt, then, the need to discover and to know and to see the unseen, was something people had been fighting with for centuries. It wasn't a feeling which just connected her to her mother. It connected her in time to explorers and travellers and ancient mariners throughout history. She felt herself blushing and lowered her head.

'So,' said Watson. 'Pigafetta joined the search for spice. Signed up his life to travel all the way round the world. A task never done before. And the crew had no idea what they'd face on their journey. Parts of the map of the world simply had "here be dragons" written on them, and the strait of water which cut through the land which the crew found, and which now has the name "the Strait of Magellan", was marked then on the map as a dragon's tail.'

'But they didn't really believe there would be dragons, did they?' said Hunter. 'Not actual fire-breathing, munching-on-people, actual dragons?'

'They did, young man. I think they really did.'

'But surely—'

'If much of the world was unexplored and unmapped, who could tell what they'd see? And anyway. There were the stories.'

Brodie moved forward in her seat.

'Stories of what could be out there in the unknown. There were the tales written by a man called Pliny the Elder who talked of giants and strange beasts. And of course, there were those who believed the tales about Prester John.'

'Who?'

'Prester John was supposed to have been a descendant of one of the magi who visited Jesus when he was born.'

'One of the three wise men?' said Sheldon, before whistling through his teeth.

'If you like,' said Watson. 'He was supposed to be a king who ruled over a kingdom of treasure and beasts. Many travellers hoped to find him on their journeys.'

Brodie jotted down notes furiously in her logbook.

# 3 searches for Magical Places...

Pliny the Elder ➡ GIANTS

strange beasts

Prester John ➡ descendant of one of the wise men!

👑 King ↪ treasure beasts

Juan de Leon ➡ fountain of youth

Power & 3.?

'And of course, just before Magellan's journey, there'd been the expedition by Juan de Leon who, many people say, set out to find the Fountain of Youth.'

Tusia looked confused.

'A fountain whose water would keep you always young,' Watson said. 'The stuff of myth and legend, of course. But you see, these myths and legends drove people to explore and to search harder and further away.' He downed the last dregs of coffee. 'Imagine if, even now, there were tales of a land where strange things lived and unusual things happened. Wouldn't we want to do all we could to find it?'

Brodie kept her head lowered. She scribbled notes frantically, trying her best to keep calm. If Watson knew what had really brought them to Yale, what would he say? If he knew what they really hoped to find, would he stop them? Would he tell them any more?

Smithies ordered extra coffee. An encouragement for Watson to continue. 'So Pigafetta was a man of learning, you say.'

'Yes. It was Pigafetta's job to record all that was seen, and all the places they passed on their journey. He kept documents and notes throughout the whole time they were away. The crew had expected the journey across the Pacific Ocean to be short. They'd no idea, then, the ocean was as big as it is.'

'How big?' said Tusia.

Watson flicked through the books in front of him. 'How about big enough to contain a quarter of all the world's water, sixty-three million square miles, and home to twenty thousand islands?'

'Fairly big then.'

'The point was, the crew had little idea about the size of the task. If they'd really known how dangerous the crossing would be, perhaps they wouldn't have attempted to make it.'

Brodie wasn't sure. If she'd known how dangerous all their work on MS 408 was going to be, would she have stopped and walked away? She knew there'd been times when she wanted to. But to actually give up?

'So sixty-three million square miles' worth of water. And Pigafetta made notes about it all.' Watson turned the coffee cup, considering what direction the conversation should take next. 'On the way, the crew captured Patagonian giants and Pigafetta spent hours trying to work out the language the giants used. He recorded their words. Made a sort of dictionary of phrases and sounds.'

'Seriously?' said Tusia. 'There really were giants?'

'Sort of. The European crew were quite short, you

=> Pigafetta <=

↓

recorded documents + notes

Pacific Ocean

a quarter of the world's water!
20,000 islands

Patagonian giants

captured

Pigafetta made ~~them~~ a dictionary of phrases + sounds

PAUL

like a code!

BB

see, average height about five foot one. But the peoples of Patagonia—'

'Where's that?' cut in Sheldon.

'At the very bottom of South America. It's called Patagonia after Magellan's word "Patagon", which means giants. And he used that word because the men there were about five foot eleven on average.'

'So they looked like giants to the European sailors then,' said Tusia.

'Exactly. The expedition captured at least three but only one survived for most of the journey across the Pacific. The crew gave the survivor the name Paul, and Pigafetta spent hours working out what he said and what it meant. He recorded it all like a code really.'

Brodie felt the skin on the back of her neck bristle. She was finding it hard to keep writing. 'So Pigafetta wrote about this code on his travels across the Pacific Ocean? He sailed past unexplored islands where they thought there were mythical beasts and on the way he wrote down a language no one knew but which looked like a code.'

Watson nodded.

It was too good to be true.

'So the books he kept notes in during the journey? You have them in the Beinecke Library?'

Every eye was on Watson. The air was charged like it is just before a storm.

He put down his coffee mug before he spoke. 'No,' he said. 'We don't.'

Kerrith spun the ring on the polished wood of the table. The flat disc on the head of the ring flashed in the light. She hadn't worn the Z Society ring for years. It hardly went with any outfit she owned and she had, after all, moved on to diamonds.

Now she watched as the ring spun round and round.

She stretched out and the ring fell on to the table, but her mind still revolved.

She remembered the day she'd first worn the ring. Hantaywee had presented it to her in a Society meeting. It meant everything to her then. An extreme honour which showed she'd been specially selected. Just like she'd been specially selected to become Director of the Black Chamber.

She cupped her fingers over the ring so it could no longer be seen.

Being the Director would give her power with few limitations. It was all she had wanted. There'd be absolutely no end to the possibilities open to her now.

* * *

'I don't understand.'

Brodie wondered how often she'd heard Tusia use those words during the months they'd been together.

'Why would Watson arrange to meet us here and give us all this information about Pigafetta if the library doesn't have a book by him?'

Watson had gone with Fabyan and Hunter to the food counter to order some lunch and Smithies was doing his best to restore calm amongst the others.

'Look, whether the Beinecke has a book or not, we've found a link,' said Brodie. 'Pigafetta was on a ship which sailed in an ocean with twenty thousand islands. One of those islands has to be Avalon, surely.'

'Twenty thousand,' said Tusia. 'Look, I'm not Hunter, but even I know that's a huge number of islands.'

'And what did Watson say?' said Sheldon. 'Sixty-three million square miles of water? It's hardly narrowing our search, is it? And besides, the whole point was, Pigafetta sailed all the way around the world, so if we really think he stopped at Avalon, then the island could be absolutely anywhere.'

Brodie waved her arms to get him to lower his voice. 'But it's Pigafetta. The name on the sword. The name in the Library of Congress. He sailed and he wrote about what he saw. He must have seen Avalon!

We've got to keep calm and get Watson to tell us more. We've got to give him time.'

After a while of watching Watson once he'd returned to their table, even Brodie was beginning to regret this sentiment.

'How the sliced pumpernickel can anyone take so long to eat two bits of bread and some meat and salad?' moaned Hunter. 'I swear to you, he's chewed that mouthful twenty-seven times.'

'Just because you don't chew your food at all,' hissed Tusia.

'But seriously, could he take any longer with his "Memoirs of a chicken" sandwich?'

Brodie doodled in her logbook as she waited. Mr Watson swallowed and then dabbed the corner of his mouth with the edge of his napkin. 'We don't have the book,' he said at last.

'So you said,' mumbled Friedman behind his hand.

'It's a shame because Pigafetta's writings are supposed to have inspired the greatest writer who ever lived.'

'Not old Shaky again,' said Hunter. 'There surely can't be a link between *him* and Pigafetta?'

Mr Watson put down his napkin. 'It's said Shakespeare used Pigafetta's writings as inspiration for one of his most famous plays.'

Brodie's writing was almost illegible as she scribbled frantically in her logbook.

'Which play?' said Smithies.

'*The Tempest*, actually.'

Brodie's pen stilled. *The Tempest* was about an island. More than that, it was the play quoted on Shakespeare's memorial in Westminster Abbey. Of all the plays. Of all the things he wrote, it was the thing chosen to be recorded for ever on his memorial. This was brilliant. But it was also impossible. 'Shakespeare used Pigafetta's work, you say, to inspire his writing. But the library doesn't have a copy of what Pigafetta wrote.'

Mr Watson's eyes darted round the room. 'I didn't say that.'

'But you said you *didn't* have the books Pigafetta wrote on the journey. You said that earlier, before you started chowing down the chicken and mustard.' Smithies glared across the table and Hunter mouthed an apology. 'It's just, you said—'

'That the Beinecke didn't have books that were written on the journey. Pigafetta's daily journal and notebooks kept by him have not survived, but these were just the raw ingredients for his writing.'

'So what happened to these ingredients?' asked Sicknote.

'Well, something referred to as *The Book* was presented by Pigafetta himself to the Emperor in Valladolid in 1522. It was recorded as being more precious than silver and gold.'

'And now? Where's that copy now?'

'No one knows,' said Watson. 'As far as history can tell us, it hasn't been preserved.'

'And the other things?'

'Extracts, summaries, papers and drawings which Pigafetta made are all talked about. But none of these survived either.'

Brodie was getting confused. 'So how does anyone know anything about what Pigafetta saw or what he did?'

Mr Watson put his hands down on the table. 'After his successful return, sometime between 1523 and 1524, Pigafetta drew up something called *The Relation*. It was the story of his adventures and four copies were made.'

'Four?' Hunter sounded like he was choking.

'Yes. One in Italian and three in French.'

'And I suppose you're going to tell us they didn't survive either,' groaned Tusia.

'Oh, no. They survived.'

'And where would they be?' said Brodie, getting a little frustrated by Mr Watson's game.

# Pigafetta's writing

The Book

Emperor, in Valladolid

Nice hat!

lost!

so are extracts, summaries, papers + drawings

so how do we know about him?!

The Relation

Italiano & Français

1 in Milan, 2 in Paris...

_1_ AT YALE!

'One in Milan, and two in Paris,' said Mr Watson.

Hunter lowered his forehead on to the table.

'But the fourth we've got in the Beinecke,' he said. '*That* is here in the library at Yale.'

'What does it say? What does it talk about? What islands does it show?'

The questions were coming thick and fast.

Mr Watson raised his hand. 'I'm afraid it's more pressing to ask about what he doesn't say and what he doesn't show.'

'What d'you mean?' said Brodie.

Mr Watson gathered his thoughts. 'We know the journey with Magellan was a trying one. It was complicated because Magellan was a Portuguese captain in charge of a Spanish fleet. There were problems on board. Mutiny even, and Magellan dealt strongly with those who'd have him overthrown as leader. But Pigafetta doesn't mention all this trauma.'

Tusia frowned.

'In the copy of *The Relation* we've got in the library, there's no mention of bad feeling or what happened to the sailors who objected to Magellan's rule.'

'You'd think someone would mention sailors being made to walk the plank,' said Sheldon.

'I'm afraid we know Magellan did more to

disobedient sailors than make them walk the plank.'

'How d'you know?' Sheldon pressed.

'There's the pilot's record of the journey.'

Sheldon was looking so confused Brodie feared he might burst.

'The pilot is the one who steers the boat. He kept records of the journey too, but they were nowhere near as detailed as Pigafetta's records written up later. The pilot's version is a collection of dates and events really. But it *does* mention the punishment of those who tried mutiny, which makes it different to Pigafetta's version. And, most importantly, the pilot's records also contradict Pigafetta's. Over important dates and places, the list by the pilot and the full account by Pigafetta are out by nearly as much as two weeks in parts.'

'And what does that tell us?'

'It would suggest one of them is wrong about the details. And I think perhaps it's Pigafetta.'

'Why d'you think that?' asked Smithies.

'Because on occasion, when writing about the last leg of the journey, Pigafetta explains he is lost for words. He seems unable to write down what he's seen at all.'

'But there were people dying, though. As they sailed. Only eighteen of them made it back. It can't have been nice for him,' said Mrs Smithies sympathetically.

'Not nice, no. But, this was all part of his job. What he signed up for. Pigafetta was taken on board to record what was seen and he doesn't keep to the deal. There are gaps. *Huge* gaps.' Mr Watson waited for his words to register. 'If I didn't know better I'd think there were things Pigafetta refused to write about because he was trying to hide them.' Mr Watson spoke quite quietly. 'If you add together the idea that all the precious notes and books from the actual journey were said to be lost, with the fact that there are differences between what he wrote and what the pilot recorded, along with all the spaces when he didn't write anything at all, then I'd say Pigafetta had a secret he was trying very hard to keep.'

# 4

# A Book Worth Far More Than 1 Silver or Gold

'We *need* to see that manuscript.' Tusia was wearing her insistent face.

'We know. But it's not going to happen,' said Sicknote with his usual negativity.

'But a document written by someone whose name is on the sword we found! Something about a journey to unknown islands and places. A book Watson's sure contains a secret.' Tusia was getting frantic now. 'We've *got* to see it.'

Hunter tried to calm her down by patting her shoulder. 'We've worked out it's important. We all get that. But what we also get is there's no way Watson, or anyone else for that matter, is going to let us go anywhere near any of the manuscripts in the Beinecke again.'

Tusia scowled like a child who'd just been told she had to have an early night.

'The Suppressors are on to us,' said Smithies. 'You heard what Watson said. They've worked out we went to look at the Voynich. We can't go back. It's too dangerous.'

Tusia stood up from the table. She pulled her arm away from Hunter's hold. 'Don't tell me what we can and can't do. Don't go on about it being dangerous. We're *this* close,' she said, pressing her thumb and index finger close together. 'This is too good a lead. We've got to follow it up.'

'OK. OK.' Smithies pulled her back down to her seat. 'But how?'

'Money,' said Sheldon.

'We've tried,' said Fabyan. 'I've chucked thousands at him just to get him to agree to meet us and tell us what he knows. Watson won't take more money.'

Hunter got up and began to pace. 'So we go for his weak spot. Something he values *over* money.'

Brodie didn't understand, but Hunter was smiling so this had to be a good thing.

'His love of *things*,' said Hunter. 'It's what made him take the money from you in the first place. You can tell he wants to be like Voynich. Have his own collection. His own cabinet of curiosities. Supposing we do a trade.'

'We give him something for his collection?' said Brodie. 'But everything we've got, we fought so hard to find. You're not suggesting we give him the map or the ring, are you?'

It was obvious from the looks cast in Hunter's direction, everyone thought this was a ridiculous idea.

'Not *keep*, but *see*,' Hunter said. 'Trade the chance to look at the Pigafetta document for the chance to see something we've found. A fair trade. Like for like.'

'And what do you suggest he'll want to see so much that he'll be prepared to risk getting us back into the Beinecke for?' asked Sicknote.

'Pigafetta's sword.'

It was clear from their faces now that Hunter's idea was maybe not so ridiculous as they'd first supposed.

'I'll phone him,' said Fabyan. 'Set it up. He's sure to go for it.'

Hunter grinned. 'See. Not just a pretty face.'

'Not even that,' said Tusia, as Fabyan moved from the bay and out into the street to make the call.

'And while we wait for Watson to say yes,' said Brodie, reaching across the table, 'I suggest we take a look at these.'

There was a general groan as Brodie gave out the various history books about Magellan's journey that Watson had brought with him as part of the agreement.

'Come on,' urged Brodie. 'Who knows what's in here that might be useful?'

'Yes. Who knows?' sighed Sheldon, flicking the pages of the rather dusty volumes with more than a fair degree of reluctance.


Brodie lost track of time. The minutes merged and the sounds of the coffee shop dulled as she turned page after page.

'Here,' said Hunter, placing a vast assortment of fruit muffins on the table as they read. 'Got to keep your vitamin C levels up. All this reading about scurvy's pretty scary.'

Brodie nibbled the edge of the nearest muffin.

'I'm not entirely sure fruit cooked with vast quantities of sugar and flour will really be much protection,' said Tusia. 'And besides, isn't the first sign of scurvy when the patient starts mumbling nonsense?' She pushed the plate away. 'If that's the case then it's far too late for you.'

Hunter crammed the last piece of his cherry muffin into his mouth sideways.

'I'm trying to concentrate,' said Brodie. 'If you don't mind.'

'No. We don't mind you concentrating,' said Hunter. 'You just tell us when—'

He didn't get to finish what he wanted Brodie to tell them.

Sheldon had stood up from the table. He pressed down hard on the open book. A tiny wisp of dust lifted.

'You OK, Fingers?'

Sheldon scrabbled for another book. He scanned down the index of the final page and then flicked through the pages before discarding the book and taking another. 'It's here. It's here,' he mumbled.

'Too late for him too, obviously,' said Tusia, folding her arms and leaning back in her chair.

Sheldon picked up another book. 'Look. Look,' he gulped.

'We are looking, mate,' spluttered Hunter through a mouthful of new muffin. 'And you're acting weird.'

'Which,' said Brodie, 'is what he does when he's found something important.'

Hunter wiped his mouth. 'Fair enough. So what you found?'

Sheldon took the final book and put it open on the table. Then he jabbed the writing and grinned.

'What am I looking at?' whispered Hunter.

Sheldon jabbed at the page again. 'The list.'

'List of what?'

'Survivors,' said Sheldon. 'Those who didn't die.'

Sicknote shivered. 'Quite amazing death rate, really,' he said. 'Two hundred and twenty-two. High by any standards. Some of them killed and then some succumbing to scurvy. A most torturous and undignified way of dying. And so totally preventable now if only they'd known.'

'It wasn't important who died,' said Sheldon.

There was a general rumble of shock around the table.

'I don't mean that in a bad way.'

'Well, that'll be a relief for the families,' said Friedman.

'I mean, it's the survivors who are important.'

'Those who are left behind,' Friedman added quietly.

Sheldon pressed on. 'Says in here that Magellan was in charge of five ships on the journey. Only one returned. It was called *The Victoria* and it sailed into Seville after having sailed all around the world, like some sort of ghost ship with only eighteen men on board.'

'And one of those men was Pigafetta,' said Smithies.

# [ Survivors ]

**Master:** Juan Sebastián Elcano

Francisco Albo
Miguel de Rodas
Juan de Acurio
} → Pilots

## Mariners:

Hernándo de Bustamante
Nicholas the Greek    Miguel Sánchez
Antonio Hernández Colmenero
Francisco Rodrigues    Juan Rodríguez
Diego Carmena

Juan de Arratia          Juan de Santandrés
Vasco Gómez Gallego      Apprentice Seaman
↑                        ↖
Able Seamen    [ Page: Juan de Zubileta

**Gunner:** Hans of Aachen
**Chief Steward:** Martín de Judicibus
**Supernumerary:** Pigafetta

'But the list of survivors shows the names of the others who returned.'

Hunter took the book. He looked more closely at the list. 'Cornish pasties and chips in gravy,' he said at last. 'Now I understand why he's so excited.'

'Could you let us in on the secret then, please?' said Sicknote.

Hunter read the list of survivors aloud. After fifteen names he read the name 'Pigafetta'. Then he paused and read two more names. 'Martin de Judicibus and Hans of Aachen.' Then he put the book down.

Sheldon smiled in satisfaction. Now they understood.


'The three Knights of Neustria,' said Tusia. 'Incredible. Part of a handful of survivors.'

'And so they must have seen Avalon together,' said Brodie. 'The three of them. Hans, the keeper of the book, *Morte d'Arthur*; Martin, the creator of the map and Pigafetta.'

'Three parts of the secret,' said Hunter. 'The perfect number.' He was juggling ideas in his brain. 'Hans had the book which drove them to look for Avalon; then Martin drew the map.'

Brodie was trying to make all the ideas slot together in her mind. 'Do you think Pigafetta wrote down what he saw when he got to Avalon and that's what MS 408 is?'

'It's totally perfect,' said Tusia. 'Didn't Mr Watson say that "a book" worth more than gold or silver was passed on to an emperor by Pigafetta when the crew got back from their travels?'

'A book which no longer exists. So history says,' laughed Sheldon.

'And we know history can be wrong,' said Brodie. 'It can leave things out. It can be skewed. So supposing the book given to the emperor *did* survive and isn't lost like the history books claim? Supposing that book was the manuscript MS 408? Supposing it was Pigafetta's secret book from his journey?'

'And supposing,' said Hunter, taking up the lead, 'the book was written in code to ensure the news about Avalon could only be read by a special few. And that other stuff Pigafetta wrote will tell us how to read it.'

'It's wonderful. It's brilliant. And it makes total sense,' yelped Brodie. 'There're two books by Pigafetta. One survives in the Beinecke and it's readable and it tells the tale of the journey. But there're gaps. There're bits missing. The writer's keeping a secret.'

'And the secret he's keeping is that he and some of the crew found Avalon,' said Tusia. 'And the story of that discovery, and all they found, was written, in

How it all fits together...

* Hans of Aachen ⟶ Morte D'Arthur
* Martin de Judicibus ⟶ (map)
* Pigafetta

saw Avalon together?

a book worth more
than gold / silver    $ £

1 book ⟶ Beinecke ⟶ readable ⟶ gaps!

coded in MS408 ◀ Avalon! ◀ secret

eventually disappeared!

HIDDEN

found again in Mondragone Castle!

code, in MS 408. This coded version of what happened is handed on to the emperor, who eventually passes it on to Emperor Rudolph and then . . .'

'Then the story of the book runs dry. It really does disappear from history. But, and this is the important bit, it isn't truly lost but simply hidden.' Sicknote had never looked so animated. 'Eventually, one day, Voynich and his friend Van der Essen stumble across the emperor's book in some dusty vault of Mondragone Castle.'

Smithies' voice was casual but his ears seemed to be pink with excitement. 'It makes sense of absolutely everything. Three men, inspired by a book written by Malory, set out to find out if Avalon exists.'

'They find it does,' said Friedman, 'but to protect the secret they break it three ways. A coded book which tells the truth. A map which shows the way. And a record of the journey which must surely make sense of the code.'

'This is it,' said Brodie, her voice burning in her throat. 'If we reunite the three pieces of the puzzle then we've found the answer. After all the searching and the hunting. If we can see Pigafetta's record of the journey then we'll be able to read MS 408. I know it.'

'And then . . . ?' Tusia's voice was just a whisper.

'What we've always promised we'd do,' said Friedman. 'We'll be able to go to Avalon.'

The door of the café swung open.

Fabyan made his way to the table. He was grinning broadly. 'So,' he said, glancing down at the pile of muffin wrappers. 'What did I miss?'

Brodie couldn't really find the words to begin to explain.

Fabyan's face fell. 'OK. Don't tell me. But what I have to know is whether you still need to see this manuscript written by Pigafetta? After a fair degree of *negotiation* with Mr Watson I've managed to set it up.'

Brodie swallowed hard.

'But if you think it'll be a waste of time, then we can always back out?' Fabyan said tentatively. 'Whatever you lot think best.'

'I've told you before, this is most irregular.'

Kerrith smiled at the man seated at the control desk. The TV monitors blinked above his head like watching eyes. 'You don't need to worry,' she said calmly.

'But there's not supposed to be contact with the . . .' he searched around for a word which would do, 'inmates.'

'No. Well. Maybe not unless the order came from the highest level.'

The man turned the thought over. 'You're telling me these orders come from the Director?'

Kerrith's smile twitched. 'Right from the top.' She placed a series of documents on the table, and a flat-headed ring on her finger glinted in the light of the electric bulb. The man scanned the documents carefully. It was clear he hadn't been chosen for the job of security by chance.

After a while he put the papers down. 'So what d'you want me to do?' His voice was lighter, his tone more respectful.

Kerrith swallowed. She'd worked it all out with extreme care. And if the Chairman was trusting her with this new role then whatever had happened in the past she had to stick to the plan. The papers on the Tyrannos Group had been really helpful and it was a relief to finally understand what she should do.

She took several new pieces of paper from her briefcase. The first had the number 408 stamped across the top. Below the title were four names. Willer, Jarratt, Longman and Fabyan. She passed the paper to the guard. 'I need these four . . .' she too searched for the word, '"inmates" dealt with.'

The guard scanned the paperwork. 'You're sure,

ma'am? It seems a little extreme.'

Kerrith fought to hold her nerve. 'The time has come,' she said. 'It must be done instantly.'

The guard put the paper down on the table as if the words it contained were so distasteful to him he wasn't sure he could bear to hold them any longer.

'But before you carry through this directive,' Kerrith added, 'I'd like you to give Hantaywee a copy of these letters. One was written many years ago. The other more recently. It should make everything very clear to her.'

'Will that be all, ma'am?'

'That should be enough,' said Kerrith, and she turned and walked towards the escalators which would take her once more up into the fresh air.

'Hey, Fingers? You look like you've just been told chocolate fountains have just been made illegal.' Hunter stuffed a handful of crisps into his mouth. 'You OK?'

'Sure. Why wouldn't I be?'

'No reason. You just seem a bit quiet, that's all.'

Brodie considered this. It was true, it had been a while since she'd heard Sheldon's harmonica and even longer since he'd played the flute.

Sheldon looked like he was going to say something,

but then thought better of it.

'Go on,' said Tusia, always the one to insist feelings were out in the open.

'It's the list of survivors,' said Sheldon at last.

'I know. Only eighteen. Seems a bit high risk if you ask me,' said Hunter.

'It's not that. It's the number of Knights. The ones who found Avalon.'

'Martin, Hans and Pigafetta,' offered Brodie. 'What about them?'

'It's just, there were three of them. Like the three brothers who set up the Beinecke and the three original Knights, Bedivere and his children. Three of them. That's all.'

He sounded like Hunter having one of his number obsessions, and Brodie reasoned this wasn't necessarily a good thing.

'It just seems to me,' Sheldon went on, 'that the three of you were in this thing together. You know, from the very start. And then I sort of tagged along. And if I hadn't joined then we might never have met Kitty. And I just wonder if . . .'

'You wonder if you belong?' said Tusia, surprise in her voice.

'I suppose.' He gave a brief nervous smile. 'It's all so neat with the number three all the time and I just wonder if I should really be here.'

Hunter gulped down his last mouthful of crisps. 'Hey, mate. Look, I know at the beginning I wasn't that keen and everything, on you joining.'

'You weren't?' said Sheldon, his cheeks reddening.

'No. I thought you knew that,' mumbled Hunter. 'But the thing is, of course you're part of the team. Honestly. It's four of us. And the other oldies.' He rubbed his hands together, a dusting of crisps crumbs falling in a tiny cloud. 'We're all in this together, you know. You have to know that.'

Friedman walked into the lobby. He stood with them but he said nothing, as if he sensed he'd interrupted something important.

'What about Kitty?' spluttered Sheldon, apparently undeterred that Friedman had joined them. 'She was here because of me. And look how that worked out.'

Brodie tried to find the right answer. 'We're all responsible for what we do, Sheldon. You're not to blame for what Kitty did. It was her decision.'

'But I thought she was on our side and really, she was like those on the boats with Magellan, the ones who led the mutinies. Pigafetta might not have talked about it. And maybe neither have we. But without me and the notes from Elgar's publisher, Kitty would never have been able to do what she did. And sometimes, when I think about it, it makes me sad.'

'It makes us sad too,' said Tusia. 'But it doesn't make us guilty. Any of us. Kitty let down the team. But you're part of that team, whether there are three people or four or more.'

Sheldon's mouth flickered into a feeble grin. But his face still looked worried.

'You agree with me, surely, Friedman, don't you?' said Tusia. 'We're all vital to this team, whatever we've done in the past.'

'Being part of the team is crucial,' he said, and his brow was furrowed as if he was thinking hard about whether to go on. 'There's something I think I should tell you all now. I know you understand that in the past I did things I wish I hadn't. Things I wish with all my heart I could change.' He hesitated. 'But I've been thinking for a while now, there was something else I should explain. Something you asked about a few months ago. About being a team.'

'OK,' Brodie said nervously.

'Guess you're troubled by the whole three parts of the secret idea, are you, mate?' Friedman said, looking sympathetically in Sheldon's direction. 'The three parts are important. Breaking things into bits means people take ages to know the truth. And that should make us think about the power of breaking things.

But there's some stuff you should also know about teams.' Brodie was sure he could hear the tremor in his voice but her father seemed determined to go on. 'When I was a little older than you lot are, I was taken to live at Station X in Bletchley. My grandparents were part of the Second Study Group trying to make sense of MS 408, and much like you, as an inquisitive child, I tried to join in. They wouldn't let us. Not properly, I mean. But we tried.'

'We?' Sheldon asked a question Brodie didn't need to ask. She knew already who'd lived with her father at Bletchley as a child. Jon Smithies and Alex Bray had been there too. As children. It was where they'd first met. Her mother, her father and Smithies. She knew this part of the story. She'd seen the photograph taken of the three of them outside the station huts.

Friedman took his wallet from his pocket and sure enough he showed the others a copy of the photograph her grandfather had shown her nearly two years ago.

'That's my mum,' Brodie said, leaning in closer to the photo. 'And Smithies, look.'

Friedman traced his thumb over the image of his own face. 'The three of us together,' he said, and he looked over at Sheldon. 'But if you think carefully, there was never really three of us at all.'

Brodie was confused. It was blatantly clear from

the photograph, there was. 'You're making no sense,' she said.

'Maybe not. And maybe now's not the time to explain.' Friedman held his hand up as Brodie began to argue. 'But it's time to warn you,' he said. 'Kitty's betrayal was a terrible, terrible thing. But don't let that weaken the ties between you. We all have a part to play in this puzzle. *All* of us. You were all chosen for your skills and your talents and the team is stronger for having each of you.'

'Is he OK?' whispered Hunter. 'We'd kind of made that point.'

Brodie shrugged.

'We're a team,' said Friedman, 'and we shouldn't leave anyone out. That's what I'm saying.'

Brodie tightened the collar of her coat. Her father was a complicated man. She knew that. She'd no idea, though, what he'd just been going on about. Still. None of that mattered now. What mattered was meeting Watson and unless they hurried they'd be late and the trade to see Pigafetta's manuscript would be off. Whatever Friedman was rambling on about would have to remain a puzzle.

It was dark. It was windy. This apparently was good news.

'Fewer security guards milling about,' said Watson. 'Still means it's extremely dangerous and I can't believe I'm doing this, but even so.'

'Has he ever asked us why we want to see the manuscript?' whispered Brodie, moving quickly along the badly lit alley.

'He's a collector of the unusual,' said Fabyan. 'He just *gets* these things.'

Brodie hurried a little further. 'And is this really the best way into the building?'

'So he says,' said Fabyan. 'Reckons he's got it all worked out.'

'Let's hope he's right,' said Granddad. 'Deportation from the United States of America would look a little bad on all our passports.'

Brodie tried to smile but she wasn't entirely sure her granddad had been joking.

The plan was relatively simple. There was no way Watson could bring the manuscript out of the library for them to see. And there was no way they could all go back into the public part of the library, with the staff now on full alert after the team's last visit. But if Pigafetta's work was down in one of the repair rooms waiting for attention, then getting a closer look was just possible. So Mr Watson had scheduled Pigafetta's manuscript for urgent repair!

The Beinecke Rare Book and Manuscript Library relied on underground buggies and carts to get around the three floors of storage stacks built under Hewitt Quadrangle. Those carts and buggies had to get into the system somehow. They did it via the goods entrance. This was the team's way back into the library and where Watson had agreed to meet them.

The curator insisted on going over the plan several times. 'Make no sound. Talk to no one. If you're discovered – run.'

Brodie thought the rules seemed pretty clear. The wind was whipping up a gale now. She was cold. And she was more than ready to move on.

Watson took a key from his pocket. He made a cross shape in front of his body like he was praying. Then he opened the door and hurried them inside.

It was the third time Brodie had been inside the underground stacks of a library. The first time she'd been with Friedman in London searching for a copy of the *Morte d'Arthur*. The second time she'd been running away from guards in the Library of Congress in Washington DC. Neither time had been a good experience. She felt a prickle of something more than excitement and wondered if the sound her heart was making was loud enough for others to hear.

Watson led the way.

It was a labyrinth. 'Does this guy know what he's doing?' hissed Hunter.

Brodie saw Granddad touch Hunter's arm quite firmly and gesture not to talk. He was obviously taking the threat of deportation very seriously.

It seemed ridiculous to be as nervous as she was and yet to be moving further and further away from the means of escape. The tunnels snaked ahead, the only light from flickering torches Watson had provided them all with at the door. Brodie thought they must look like a strange procession of glow-worms snaking through the dark.

After what seemed an eternity, the front of the line stopped.

There was a scraping noise. A key in a lock and then a door opened.

Beams of torches swirled and connected to give the room an orange glow.

Brodie could see the room was filled with boxes and files.

Watson hurried them inside the storeroom and shut the door. He switched on a single overhead bulb. Then he took a box from the shelving to his left and lifted the lid.

'Pigafetta's manuscript,' he said, holding the swaddled document like a child. 'Now show me the sword.'

# 5

# A Trade of Ostrich Eggs and Egyptian Mummies

Summerfield sat one side of the desk; Kitty the other. Papers filled the space between them. 'This is everything. From the situation board, from Friedman's flat, from reports in the field. We just need you to help us fill in the gaps.'

'I can't—'

Summerfield was growing weary. 'We've been through this, Miss McCloud. I'm afraid you're no longer in a position to tell us what you can and can't do. You've no choice but to help us. Ask yourself these simple questions: Is there anyone else in the world you matter to now? Anyone you can turn to? Can you really go home, knowing how you betrayed those who trusted you and that we at the Chamber will be tracking your every move?' He paused for just one moment. 'You understand what happens to those the Chamber have an interest in, don't you, Kitty?'

Kitty's shoulders began to shake.

'We're your only friends in the world now.' He couldn't help but sneer at the end of his phrase, then he leant forward and pushed his hands down hard on the desk. 'Start talking or we can make things very difficult for you. Am I making myself clear?'

Kitty scanned the topmost layer of papers. She could see photos of the team from Station X taken by grainy security cameras – in hotels, in New York, in London. Her fingers trembled as she picked up the topmost photograph. It was of Leicester Square. The statue of Shakespeare clearly visible, the team grouped around him.

Summerfield grabbed the photo from her. 'There's something here? A detail we missed?'

Kitty shook her head. Her eyes were red. 'I don't know. I keep telling you.'

'We're interested in connections they may have rejected. Or not managed to see the use of yet. We need you to try!'

Kitty looked up at the photo that Summerfield flapped in front of her and she could feel the colour rush to her cheeks.

Kerrith coughed gently from the corner of the room. 'That's enough,' she said.

Summerfield's eyes were bulging. 'But, ma'am. We can't possibly stop now. The girl's told us nothing.'

'I said, that's enough,' pressed Kerrith.

Miss Vernan had been much easier to work with when she was distracted. This renewed commitment was irritating.

'I'll take it from here,' Kerrith added, moving closer to the desk.

Kitty began to sob.

Kerrith leant forward and her voice was sharp. 'Miss McCloud needs a little reminder of our previous discussion. She needs to be sure she's focusing on who her friends really are.'

Kerrith smiled in Summerfield's direction.

He stood. Then he pushed the photograph deep into his jacket pocket before leaving the room.


Mr Smithies moved to the front of the group. Under the light of the single bulb it was difficult to see him clearly but Brodie watched as he reached inside his coat and drew out a long, thin bundle of cloth. Then, moving slowly, he unwrapped it so the covering fell away. He straightened his arm and held

Pigafetta's sword in the air.

The return from the Blue Ridge Mountains had been so muddled, and the devastation they found back at Riverbank so difficult to understand, that for a while the sword, like Martin de Judicibus's map, had remained untouched. Somehow, spending time looking at what the team had found, while the Suppressors were plotting the death of their friend, seemed wrong. Now it seemed incredible they'd not spent longer looking at the treasure they'd found.

The stockroom had been almost totally dark except for the bare bulb. Now a stronger light seemed to shine. Light from the sword.

The blade was fairly short and wide, like the blade of a dagger, pointed at the tip. As Smithies moved, Pigafetta's name glistened in the light across the flattened surface. The hilt was gold, the quillions and pommel studded with stones like the one which shone in Brodie's locket. They sparkled blue then pink then lilac, colour flowing through them like water.

'Elfin Urim?' whispered Tusia.

Brodie nodded.

'What?' hissed Sheldon.

Brodie stepped in closer to explain. 'One of the Knights of Neustria, Alfred Lord Tennyson, wrote about a sword from Avalon. He talked about the elfin

Urim on the hilt. It was a clue we used to solve the Firebird Code before you joined us,' she added. 'The code which began this whole adventure.'

Sheldon looked impressed.

'Tennyson said men of the world could be blinded by the beauty of the sword,' added Hunter. 'Looks to me like he might have been predicting the effect a sword of Avalon would have on our Mr Watson.'

Brodie turned to see where he looked. Mr Watson was still clutching to the bundle he'd taken from the box, but his eyes were as wide as saucers and his mouth was hanging open.

'Mr Watson.' Smithies was whispering, maybe scared that if he spoke too loudly, the man would drop the book he held. 'Mr Watson. Should we swap?'

'What? Yes. Quite. Swap. Yes.'

If Brodie hadn't known better, she'd have been sure the man in front of her was having some sort of 'episode'. She wouldn't have been surprised if, at any moment, he'd slipped to the ground in a cold, dark faint. Instead, Mr Watson stepped forward and held out his bundle. Smithies moved quickly. Then, once his friend had the book, he lowered the sword and let Mr Watson take it. 'Exquisite,' the curator mumbled. 'The craftsmanship is truly out of this world.'

Brodie waited to see if anyone would say anything.

Sicknote was looking nervy. 'If we're not careful, he'll begin to ask too much,' he whispered. 'We need to get on with this before he gets suspicious and starts asking questions.'

Mr Watson's mouth was now so wide open, Brodie was pretty sure it would be a very long time before he asked anything at all, but Sicknote, gulping on his inhaler, seemed very keen to move on.

They huddled as they'd done around MS 408. Smithies took the pair of gloves that were wrapped with the manuscript and slipped them on. Then he put the book down on the upturned crate in the centre of the room, so everyone could see. Behind them, Mr Watson looked at the sword, and the light from the blade burned.

Pigafetta's manuscript was listed as MS 351, also part of the general collection, but Brodie thought it would have been impossible for two manuscripts to have looked more different. MS 408 had been tatty and scruffy, its edges uneven and stained. This book was clean and regular in shape and it was bound with a perfect scarlet leather cover, bordered with intricate golden patterning. It was beautiful in an obvious sort of way.

Smithies turned the cover. The inside was bright with swirling orange and red patterns twisting and curling like flames. Across the middle of the inside cover was the university stamp like the one in MS 408. '*Lux et Veritas*,' Brodie read again to herself. 'Light and truth.'

Smithies turned the pages. Endpapers of white followed. Clean and unscuffed. This manuscript had been treated with care. But on the sixth page, someone had written notes by hand, down the page and in the corners across it.

'It's in French, I think,' said Smithies.

Granddad shuffled closer and peered in.

'Well?' said Brodie.

'Give me a mo.'

Her granddad understood her impatience. They all did. They wanted to know what it said. And they wanted to know quickly. 'It's something about how this is the manuscript which was presented to the Grand Master of Rhodes.'

'Who the McFlurry was he?' hissed Hunter.

No one knew, but Tusia leant forward and, using Brodie's phone, she began to take photos of the pages. They'd talked before about how Mr Watson might not like this and how he might bang on about light levels and possible damage to the book. As it was, Mr Watson didn't notice. He was busy with the sword.

Photos of the pages had been Tusia's idea. If they

couldn't take the manuscript with them they needed records of what they saw. If this manuscript was as important as they hoped, and it was really part of the puzzle, they needed all the photos they could take.

Smithies moved forward again, lifted the flyleaf and turned.

The next page made Brodie's heart thump.

Stamped clearly and boldly across the following page, and wreathed with leaves, were three stars. Perhaps the three Knights of Neustria. Pigafetta, and Martin and Hans.

But more important than that – more exciting and more powerful – was another image.

Strong and elegant, and lit for a moment in the brilliant flash of the phone, was a picture of a phoenix.

Summerfield turned the key in the lock and swung open the door. The light clicked on automatically. It illuminated a corridor of filing cabinets. Personal records deemed too sensitive to store on computer.

He'd been too patient, he decided. Kerrith losing the plot was one thing. Her rearranging the way things should go was something else and he needed to know why.

He shut the door behind him and tried to walk without making a sound.

The final cabinet was the one he needed. The very lowest drawer. He took the file labelled 'KERRITH VERNAN' and rested it on top of the cabinet. It was time to understand his boss more fully.

There was the usual stuff. ID photos, date of birth, length of service. Nothing remarkable. And then he found it. The section that made everything clear.

The photograph was old and tattered, damaged in one corner. It showed two women, laughing and smiling at the camera. One looked a lot like Kerrith. Younger and softer though. And in fact Kerrith's name was printed across the bottom of the photograph. The other name was harder to read.

Summerfield flicked to the next page. This time one face looked out from the photograph. The same woman with the unusual name again, that much was clear, but her face was aged and lined now. Underneath it an official stamp. *Site Three Detainee. Indefinite.*

Summerfield flicked back to the first photo. Kerrith knew this woman? A woman now held prisoner by Level Five.

He closed the file and tried to calculate what this meant. And for the moment he had absolutely no idea.

Tennyson had been right. Mr Watson was totally blinded by the sword. It was as if he knew his time was precious and he wanted to store in his mind the memory of the weight of the blade and the movement of the rippling gems against the gold.

Team Veritas took photos to remember.

Smithies turned the pages with his gloved fingers and Tusia angled Brodie's phone to record each shot. They worked with speed and diligence even when Brodie called out for them to slow down and let her see more clearly.

'We've got to do this quickly, B,' insisted Hunter. 'It's no good stopping and reading when at any moment we're going to have to leave. We've got to get shots of everything.'

Brodie understood this. But she also knew that as the pages flicked past she felt a sense of panic as parts of the story were hurried over or ignored. This was the book which could have all the answers and she wanted to see them.

But it wasn't as if she could read the words as they turned quickly past her eyes. The writing was in French and, however good Miss Carter had been at covering the basics with them back at school, Brodie hadn't really got much further than being able to name the parts of the body and ask the way to the bookshop. She hoped her granddad was up to the task of translation. They were depending on him totally.

The written pages of the book were covered in tiny writing. Brodie could see that every now and then there were illuminated letters, and what looked like chapter headings were written in red or blue italics in places across the script. There were notes too, written neatly in italics in the margins.

Down the length of the pages were words arranged in columns, like lists. It made it look like the word and its meaning had been set out like a dictionary entry.

And there were maps.

Interspersed between the pages of writing were pages edged with golden borders. Land was coloured dark brown and the sea blue, flecked with darker blue and gold to show the waves. Across each land mass was a tiny picture of a scroll where Pigafetta had written the name of the island.

'Twenty-three,' said Hunter decisively, when Tusia had taken the final photograph.

'What?' Brodie could not believe that when looking at such a beautifully put-together manuscript, Hunter could bang on about numbers.

'There's twenty-three of them.'

'Twenty-three what?'

'Maps.' He sighed. 'Can you imagine a sea so big that in order to draw the islands you pass, you have to draw twenty-three separate maps to include them all?'

'That's quite a lot of islands,' said Tusia, pressing the phone to check she'd recorded every page. 'And he's named them all, look, even though many of them had never been mapped before.'

Tusia stopped. She held the phone still. Then she pressed the touch-screen frantically.

'Don't tell me you pressed "delete" instead of "save",' said Sicknote. 'Happens to me all the time. I had some brilliant photographs of some rather severe bruising on my shin which I wanted to show my doctor, but of course, when I got to the surgery I'd wiped the lot. Tragedy.'

Brodie doubted it actually was a tragedy but she was concerned about Tusia. Her face was pinched, showing she was concentrating hard. Her finger still prodded ferociously at the phone. Then she stopped.

'Knew it,' she said. 'Absolutely knew it. It's incredible. It's just so odd.'

'Talking about herself again,' whispered Hunter, before Tusia thrust the phone rather inelegantly in his direction.

'Look.'

'What am I looking at?' yelped Hunter.

'I don't know,' said Tusia defensively. 'That's the point.'

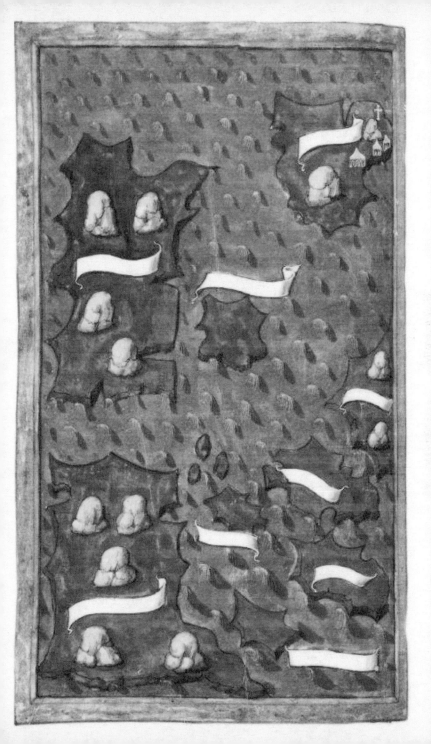

'What you on about, Toots?'

Tusia took the phone again and thrust it this time in Brodie's direction. 'You have a look,' she said. 'What d'you see?'

Brodie peered down at the screen. 'Islands,' she said. 'Lots of islands.'

'And what are they called?' continued Tusia.

Brodie grimaced. 'We've been over this. Until Granddad gets to work with the translation, then I can't tell.'

Tusia pulled a face. 'Well, the best translator in the world would have trouble with those names,' she said. 'No offence, Mr Bray, and everything, but look.'

Brodie's granddad peered in closely. 'Ahh, a little tricky.'

'Will someone please tell me what's difficult about the names,' said Sheldon, reaching for the phone. 'Oh. I see.'

Tusia folded her arms and Brodie moved in nearer to Sheldon to have another look.

Now she understood.

Not a single island on this particular map had a name. The scrolls were there, showing Pigafetta had intended to write them in, but each carefully drawn name-plate was empty.

'What page?' said Hunter.

Tusia looked up.

'What page are those islands?'

Tusia looked at the display and read off the screenshot number. 'Page thirty-five,' she said.

Mr Smithies turned the pages of the book and held the pages of the manuscript open.

'Nine,' said Hunter quietly.

'No. Thirty-five. He's found the page. Look.' Sheldon was gesturing to the open manuscript.

'I have looked,' said Hunter. 'That's why I said *nine*.' The obstinate expression didn't leave his face. 'I'm not talking about the page number. I'm talking about the number of unnamed islands.'

'Oh.'

'And there are nine of them.'

'And why's that important?' pressed Sheldon, looking baffled again.

'Because of the number of islands drawn in MS 408.'

Brodie remembered the page of islands. Adam's favourite page. The extending page which stretched out of the manuscript and revealed the islands linked by causeways.

Hunter smiled. 'There were nine.'

\* \* \*

Hantaywee Fabyan folded the piece of paper. The creases were worn now, thinning to the point of tearing. She didn't need to re-read the words. She knew every one by heart. But it helped her to hold the paper in her hand.

Today was the day.

She'd never have thought Kerrith was capable of such a thing. She'd been her very best friend. Even so, it was hard to believe.

But now, today, just as the letter had said, it would all be over. For her, for Evie, for Miss Longman and Mr Willer.

She was scared.

Kitty passed Kerrith a slice of carrot cake. It had been a long time since she'd eaten cake. She rocked the fork backwards and forwards on the plate and sweat prickled on her forehead.

Kitty looked nervous too. Kerrith couldn't blame her. The girl was obviously concerned about the plan. But Kerrith was, as always, resolute and determined. Summerfield had understood things from the internal memo she'd sent him. Keeping the young betrayer close was important. Kitty would weaken eventually, Kerrith had told him. Or she'd remember. Kerrith would have access, then, to all the details the Black Chamber needed. As new Director she should be the first to make connections from the details a rejected member of the team from Station X could bring her. They just needed to be patient.

The ring on the doorbell was unexpected.

Kerrith put the fork on the edge of the plate and pressed the serviette to her lips.

'Shall I get it?' asked Kitty.

Kerrith folded the serviette in half and waited. Her stomach spasmed completely when she saw the Chairman.

'I'm not in the business of making house calls,' he said, filling the space in the doorway with his crisp grey suit.

Kerrith stumbled to her feet. The fork fell on to the floor, spreading icing on the carpet. She didn't even look down.

'I've come to make a few things clear,' he said.

Kerrith muttered something about coffee, or something stronger, and the Chairman batted her suggestion away.

'Miss Vernan, there's been some developments. At Site Three. Some unpleasantness.' He was choosing his words carefully. 'It seems to me, the events unfolded as a result of the Director.'

Kerrith felt her forehead prickle again with sweat. 'I can—'

The Chairman held up his hand. 'No need to explain, Miss Vernan. We were concerned about Channey's commitment as Director for a while.'

Kerrith was confused. Did he think the past Director had issued the command?

'I've just come to talk to you about how history works, Miss Vernan. How thorough the art of suppression we practise can be. May I?' He gestured towards the sofa and Kerrith nodded for him to sit.

'It's all about control. That's what it comes back to. And the point is, Miss Vernan, we are the ones in control. Do you understand what I'm saying?'

Kerrith wasn't really sure she did.

'Tyrannos. That's the key. It's what ties us all together and makes all we do fit into place. The work of governments across the world, working with one accord to ensure that what *has* to be done, *is* done.' He looked agitated. 'The Director worked well for the Chamber. His commitment was rarely in doubt. But at the end of the day, he took out only one operative during his time on the case of 408. History, if it were to judge him, would cast him as weak. We've recently received medical reports about his death. Seems he was taken out by something small and insignificant. He

116

made a mistake, Miss Vernan, and the art of suppression has little room for mistakes.'

Kerrith could feel her heart beating frantically in her throat.

'I want you to take a look at these, if you will.' He passed her a file of papers. 'I suppose you could say this is what our endgame is.'

The hairs on Kerrith's arms stood up.

'In life we control stories, Kerrith. And even in death, there needs to be control. Mistakes cannot be tolerated. Don't think that just when people die, there's suddenly a right for their story to be told. "Cradle to the grave" is the scope of our work of suppression. It's best you understand that.'

Kerrith's foot caught against the fork on the ground. There was a streak of white icing on the carpet.

The Chairman stood up. He took the serviette, bent down and wiped the stain away. 'Mistakes, like stories, can be "vanished" if they need to be.'

'It feels wrong,' said Smithies.

'Bit late for that,' said Friedman, 'after all we've done. I know we're in a storeroom of a very important library taking photographs of a very precious document. But we've done worse. Much worse. It's not that wrong when you think about the end result.'

Smithies groaned. 'I'm not talking about what we're doing.'

'But you said it felt wrong.'

'And that's what I meant,' blurted Smithies. 'It *feels wrong*.'

Brodie had no idea what he was talking about.

'The page,' he snapped. 'The page feels wrong.'

He took off one of his gloves and passed it to Tusia. 'You're the "shape and space" one. You tell me.'

Tusia took the glove and slipped it on. She moved closer to the packing case. Then she put her hand tentatively down on page thirty-five. Nine islands like the ones drawn in MS 408.

'I can see some buildings,' she said. 'Look, on one of the islands. And a cross.'

'Maybe that shows the castle,' suggested Brodie, as Tusia continued to run her hand along the page.

'Which must mean, surely, this map shows Avalon just like the map in MS 408. It's all fitting together,' said Mrs Smithies. 'Like we hoped it would.' Her eyes sparkled and Brodie thought how strange it was to see her suddenly full of excitement. Since spending time at Riverbank and being needed by them, she looked young again, somehow.

'But do you feel it yet?' urged Smithies. 'It feels wrong, doesn't it?'

Tusia frowned and ran her finger along the edge of the page.

'Well?' Smithies was almost frantic.

'It's too thick,' said Tusia. 'More than double the thickness of the other pages.'

'Double the thickness of a page of paper,' laughed Hunter. 'Exactly how thick is a single sheet?'

'Well, not as thick as this, obviously,' snapped Tusia.

Brodie tried to calm the mood. 'So what does that mean?'

Tusia was breathing in deeply as if trying to inhale an answer. 'No idea. But it's odd, isn't it? The page we find the most fascinating, the page we think is so important, is thicker than the others.'

'So the page is different,' said Hunter. 'Like the one in MS 408.'

Tusia didn't move. 'You're right,' she said.

'I am?'

'You are! I know it doesn't happen often, but you are!'

Hunter looked embarrassed and Tusia lifted her hands from the manuscript. 'What was special about our favourite page in MS 408?'

'It had nine islands on it,' said Sheldon.

'And?'

'There was the castle,' said Brodie.

'And?'

'It grew bigger,' said Hunter.

Brodie turned to face him. He'd said some crazy things during their work on various codes but this had to be up there with his most ridiculous statements. 'Grew bigger? Are you totally nuts?'

'No more so than you,' said Hunter, which she supposed reluctantly was probably close to the truth.

'It stretched out, didn't it?' Tusia explained. 'It extended from the book. Like Hunter said, it grew bigger. That's what made it special. And so. Perhaps,' she was looking nervous again, 'this page feels too thick because it actually extends. Maybe there's more of the page, folded in.'

Brodie was finally following the logic. 'Well, is there a flap?'

Tusia shook her head.

'So how would the page extend? How would we make it bigger?'

'If the page was made to grow bigger then maybe it was folded over and sewn in when the book was bound,' suggested Sheldon.

'So how do we make it bigger?' said Brodie again.

'We cut it,' said Tusia quietly.

Sicknote began coughing. He thumped his chest

120

and his eyes began to water. 'We do what?'

'Slice along the centre fold,' said Tusia relatively calmly. 'When the book was put together the pages were bound in the middle. If we slice carefully along the fold we should be able to lift open the flap.'

This explanation did little to calm Sicknote. 'We've cut up copies of the *Morte d'Arthur*, we've sliced open covers of unique books housed at Shugborough Hall and now,' he could barely finish his sentence, 'now you want us to go slicing open pages of a manuscript put together in 1523. It's madness, I tell you.'

Tusia folded her arms defensively. 'Maybe it is. But we did all those things with the other books and we found answers.'

'But don't you think there's a chance our luck might have run out in that department?' groaned Sicknote.

'Or don't you think it would just show we're following the links like you always said we should,' retorted Tusia.

Sicknote looked positively green.

'The page is too thick,' Tusia said again. 'I think that means there's writing hidden inside a folded flap. I think that makes sense and I think we'd be mad to miss this chance.'

Sicknote had taken a seat on the floor and Granddad

was fanning him with the spare glove. 'How?' Sicknote gulped.

'How what?' said Tusia.

'How will you do it?' He couldn't bring himself to look up.

Tusia scanned the room. They'd hardly come prepared with cutting implements and yet . . .

Sicknote lowered his head into his hands.

'Mr Watson,' said Tusia quietly. 'If it's all right with you, we'd rather like our sword back now.'

To say it was easy to persuade Mr Watson they knew what they were doing was a bit of an overstatement. His reaction made one of Sicknote's swoons look very undramatic. He began to splutter uncontrollably about his job and his future and at one point Mrs Smithies had to slap him firmly round the cheek to stop hysteria setting in.

In the end it was the Egyptian mummy and the ostrich eggs that did it.

Fabyan promised he would have these artefacts, and a few others, shipped over from Bletchley and that as long as Mr Watson promised to say nothing to anyone about what they'd done, he could have them. Mr Watson still sobbed a little, but he did nothing more to stop them.

'We're just letting the document be all it can be,' said Brodie. 'It was destined to one day do this and all we're doing is letting it reach its full potential.' She went on a bit about flightless birds having the courage to finally take to the air, and how eventually the phoenix had to fly higher than the dragon. These stories and images thrilled her, but had little effect on Mr Watson. Offers of more money from Fabyan finally shut him up completely.

Tusia had the steadiest hand. She took the sword and she pointed the tip into the centre of Pigafetta's manuscript. The stones on the pommel glowed more brightly like in the cave in the Blue Ridge Mountains. It looked to Brodie like the sword was being placed back in its scabbard, or as if somehow it was being returned to Avalon. It didn't look wrong. Brodie felt no fear. This, she knew, was what they needed to do.

Tusia cut at the binding. One by one, she sliced through each stitch. Then she stopped and she passed the sword to Sheldon.

Then, with her hands re-gloved, she lifted the pages from the centre of the manuscript. The page flapped back on itself. Tusia smoothed it flat. Then she lifted the bottom edge. Another flap.

The page with the nine unnamed islands had

grown. It stretched out of the book like the page in MS 408.

Across every millimetre of the extended page was writing which had been hidden from the world for hundreds of years.

# The Words of Babel

'Got one.'

Fabyan stood in the doorway of the hotel bedroom. He held a laptop. Brodie's smartphone was connected by a cable. He balanced the two on the end of the bed and flicked through the screenshots of Pigafetta's book taken in the Beinecke Rare Book and Manuscript Library.

For a moment Brodie didn't want to look closely at the enlarged images on the screen. She knew when she did, it would somehow be over, and she wasn't sure how that would feel.

They'd spent so many hours over the last year or more, holed away in hotel bedrooms and huts at Station X looking for answers to one question. What did MS 408 say? They'd followed so many twists and turns, puzzles and clues, and it had all been about that single question. What did the glyphs and the squiggles in a book which was five hundred years old and had never been read actually mean?

Brodie felt the excitement might explode inside her.

There might be more twists and more confusion and it might be difficult, but she knew the photos of Pigafetta's writing must and would make sense of MS 408. Everyone in the room believed that, she could feel it. That was why, after all the setbacks and the pain and the dramas, they hadn't given up. They'd *known* they would find meaning in the confusion of the swirls and squiggles. It hadn't been a hope. It had been a certainty. That was what made the Third Study Group different from the Second and different from the First. And different from everyone else who'd ever tried to make sense of the Voynich Manuscript.

Total and utter belief.

They organised the photographs of the pages of the book into two folders on the screen. One, the known story of Pigafetta's adventures on the high seas. The other, a smaller set. Four photos in total. The folded pages of the manuscript they'd cut free with Pigafetta's sword.

Granddad took a deep breath. 'Ready?' he said.

Brodie had the logbook open. Her pen poised.

It was finally time to read Pigafetta's secret.

Mr Bray sat down then lifted the laptop on to his knees and began to read. His eyes, old now, darted backwards and forwards frantically as they scanned each word and phrase. His French was broken and stumbling, but Brodie wrote down every word. Everyone else sat still. Unmoving until he read the final sentence. Brodie put down the pen.

The air crackled.

'Shall I read it through?' Brodie said.

She didn't need their answer before she began.

*'And so the hidden place of the real story of our journey has been uncovered. I wonder if this missive was found by chance or deliberate and determined choice. I shall never know, for I am sure that by the time this secret is unearthed I will be long gone from this place. But I retire of this worldly realm having discovered far more riches and wonders than I ever dreamed possible to have found. And this, dear reader, is the explanation of how you will find the true and complete story of my voyage, to a world beyond my own.*

*'It was Hans who first told me of Avalon. Hours and days at sea brings men close but it was a while*

*before he trusted me enough to share. He talked of a book of myth and legend, a tale of daring knights and magical swords. Readers believed the story to be the stuff that dreams concoct but Hans knew the truth of the tales. He was a member of an order of the valiant Knights of Neustria, descendants of the gallant Sir Bedivere, and he explained to me the order's obligation to search for, and protect on discovery, the realm of Avalon. Alone at sea, I was unsure of the validity of his words, the accuracy of his predictions, but I write here to tell you that all he spoke about and prophesied is true. Avalon exists. I, dear reader, have been there.*

*'Twas whilst sailing across an ocean far larger than man can imagine that Hans and I and an honourable fellow Martin de Judicibus made landfall at the hallowed ground. The wonders that befell us are too incredible to imagine and yet I have tried, dear reader, to convey the beauty and the splendour of what we saw in a document other than this. But in order to maintain the honour of the Knights of Neustria I record my thoughts and discoveries not in MY native tongue but in THE native tongue. The one language that if we troubled to remember would bind and unify us all and bring to us a power and a strength unparalleled.*

*'Twas the Patagonian giant, Paul, who shared the words I needed with me. A man of stature of heart and mind as well as body. For his is the language of Babel. The logos. The original words that flowed through us all, and with much diligence and faithful regard for the rules and habits of his speaking, I record my story in his tongue for all who truly seek to read.*

*'I grow weary and am sure that the world who has long forgotten the language of Babel will find my scribbling and my story strange and alien to them. But know this. I record the truth of Avalon and those who truly seek will find.'*

Brodie put down the logbook. She sat on the edge of the bed and she wrapped her arms around her knees.

'What does it all mean?' said Hunter.

'That all those months ago, right at the very beginning of it all, back at Station X when we first began to search and ask questions about MS 408, Tusia was right,' said Smithies.

Tusia looked distinctly startled. 'I was?'

Smithies nodded. 'You said perhaps MS 408 was written in some weird forgotten language.'

'I did?'

'And we were sure that was wrong, because the

document had to be in code. Being in code made sense of everything else we knew.'

'But,' Sheldon took up the thread of her thought, 'in the end, both things were true.'

'They were?'

Brodie let her hands slide down her knees. 'So MS 408 was written, by Pigafetta, to tell the tale of his adventures in Avalon. He knew it was important to the Knights of Neustria to keep what he'd written a secret. He knew the story had to be protected and so he wrote it in code using a language no one else but he and a giant from Patagonia knew.'

'It's like in the war,' said Granddad. 'With the Navajo code talkers.'

'Excuse me?'

'The code talkers were Native Americans who sent messages in their own language and no one who intercepted the messages could understand what was said. The language was the code. That's how it worked.'

'And so the language of MS 408,' said Hunter, 'was the original language everybody spoke. What did Pigafetta call it?'

'The language of Babel,' said Sicknote.

'See, that's the bit that gets me confused,' said Tusia. 'What's Babel?'

Smithies stood up. 'Time for a story,' he said, winking at Brodie. 'The Bible tells us that millennia ago there were all these people and they could all understand what everyone said. And they got together and they built a fabulous tower. It was enormous and really impressive and according to the story, the Creator looked down and saw the tower and he began to get a bit worried.'

'Worried? About a tower?' Sheldon was trying to keep up.

'Well, it showed how well people could work together and build things from their imaginations and that scared him because he realised if people could imagine incredible things, and they could all work together, that would make them really powerful.'

'And this worried him, why?'

'Think of the bad things people could do if they wanted to. And if they worked together.' He let the thought hang in the air a little. 'It's like the fire Prometheus stole. Fire can do great and terrible things. The fire of the imagination can be wild and scary.'

'But it can do good things too though, can't it?' said Sheldon. 'We talked about that before. How fire can cleanse and make new things grow. So with this one language there would have been good things too. Right?'

'Yes, but in the story, the Creator was worried about the bad. And so he mixed things up. He made it difficult for people to understand each other and he spread them out across the world.'

'And that's how different languages began?' said Hunter.

'So the story says. And it makes sense, doesn't it? Explains why people all across the world speak differently.'

'Could do,' said Hunter.

'But this Patagonian giant,' went on Smithies, 'that Magellan's crew captured and took on to their boat. He somehow knew this language of Babel. The first language. The one which linked us all.'

Hunter was catching on. 'And so, while they were sailing along, he must have shared this language with Pigafetta.'

'And then Pigafetta used it to write the story of Avalon,' confirmed Smithies.

'And so,' said Sicknote, 'the coded writing of MS 408 is in a language we should have all known.'

'And more than that,' said Smithies. 'It's a language we all do know, somehow. Babies "babble", don't they? It's just chance really that the Hebrew word for Babylon, where this story took place, sounds like "babble". Coincidence or not, the word works well.

Babies don't have words or sentences but they make babbling sounds and those sounds tell us what they need. I know adults don't always understand, but it's how it works. How babies first talk. Until we, as older people, make things confused and we give them different words.'

Granddad looked sort of wistful. 'It's beautiful,' he said. 'When you think about it. A code which goes back to the very first language spoken.'

Hunter's brow was furrowed as he racked his brain. 'Didn't that guy Zimansky say that?'

Friedman looked incredibly confused but Fabyan beamed. 'In my grandfather's papers,' he said. 'The magazines he kept. There was a whole article about MS 408 and this guy called Zimansky said he thought MS 408 was written in a *universal* language. And now we know it really was. The original universal language.'

'And there was that quote,' said Tusia, pacing up and down. 'In the Library of Congress. Remember?'

No one made it clear they did so she drove on anyway.

'*Out of the many there is one.*'

Brodie took a deep breath. 'I remember.'

'And then there was all that stuff at the Tower of the Winds,' said Sheldon. 'One *tower*,' he explained,

# The Language of Babel

★{Out of the many there is one!}★

Tower of
Babel

Tower of the Winds →

only the
North wind

one original
language

*stone of Avalon*
*Elizabeth*

Z Society

⊙handle with care

emphasising his words. 'Like your Tower of Babel. And remember how there were pictures around the top. And they should have been of all four winds. But there was only one. The North Wind. Do you remember?'

'Out of the many there is one,' said Tusia again. 'It fits beautifully.'

'And so all along,' said Brodie, 'we should have been searching for the one language, the original language, the one we had in the beginning.' Something clicked inside her. 'Like I always had the stone of Avalon and I always had Elizebeth as my middle name. What we needed from the very beginning was what we always had.'

Sicknote climbed heavily to his feet. He stood in the middle of the room. 'This is all lovely,' he said. 'It all sounds great but I still don't know how this will work. I still don't understand what you think we need to do.'

'You were never sure, were you, Oscar?' said Smithies. 'From the very beginning I had to try and persuade you that children would be right for this project because they wouldn't know what it was good to see and what it wasn't. They weren't scared. That was the point of it all. And they've proved it every step of the way. In the River Wye at Chepstow, on Fuller's lighthouse on the cliffs, in the caves of the Blue Ridge Mountains, they've found the answers. And I think, after all this time, I know now, how this will work.'

'Well, I don't, Jon. You need to make it clear.'

Smithies pressed his hands together, making it look like he was praying. 'Do you remember the Z Society, Brodie? And what happened to you on the steps of Virginia University? That girl knew. She could see it when you collapsed.'

Brodie remembered.

'She was scared a part of you was dying. A part of you which could look at the world and see the story.' He began to pace. 'You know when a baby is first born, if you hold it under the arms, it can raise its legs and step. It can walk in the air and knows how to move its feet. Hold that same baby in the water and it can swim. It knows how to hold its breath. But after a time, those skills are lost. They disappear.'

Sicknote looked perplexed. 'What are you talking about, Smithies? You're making no sense.'

Smithies' grin widened. 'I'm making no sense because I'm an adult.' He folded his arms. 'Do you understand what I'm trying to say, Brodie? Have you worked out the secret of how to read MS 408?'

Brodie lifted her head. She looked around the

room. They were waiting. All of them waiting, watching and longing for her to make sense of it all. And she knew then, she could. Pigafetta's letter and the language of MS 408. She could make sense of it now.

And most importantly, if only she'd known at the very beginning, she'd always been able to.

Brodie took the facsimile of MS 408 and held it towards the light. She thought of the beginning of the whole adventure and she remembered how Van der Essen had finished his Firebird Code. *Handle with care*. That phrase made her smile. Months ago, those words had only been read to help them find the right place in the Royal Pavilion. Now the words meant so much more.

She pressed the book carefully with her fingers. It felt warm. She remembered all the times she'd held it before and longed to know what it said. This time the warmth from the book burned not just in her hands but in a place deep inside her. She knew what she should do.

She remembered how she'd felt when she'd sat with Hunter weeks before at Tandi's grave. Adam had been with them then. He'd looked at her in a way that showed he was totally sure she could make sense of the words the manuscript contained. He'd believed in her ability to break the code and to find the castle. He'd looked at her as a child and known somehow she would do it.

And so Brodie opened the manuscript.

For a moment, Brodie was no longer in the hotel bedroom with her circle of friends. She was somewhere else. Inside a memory. It was as if she'd travelled back in time and she wasn't scared or even surprised. She stood outside of herself and looked down. She was a tiny child again, maybe only three years old. She wasn't alone. Her granddad was there, looking much younger, and there was a beautiful woman, who, she realised with a jolt, was her mother, and she was sitting beside him. Her mother held a storybook and the younger version of Brodie climbed on to her mother's lap as she turned the pages and began to read. And the younger Brodie leant forward and she peered at the words and she connected the shapes and the squiggles on the printed page with the story her mother told. She became part of the story. She laughed and she giggled. Her grandfather, too, joined in with the tale, adding voices and jokes as the words on the page combined with the words they shared, weaving an invisible shield around them. Brodie remembered the power of story. The feeling of an imagined world being set free from the page.

And then the vision Brodie saw shifted once again. This time she saw three new figures. Men she didn't recognise, but men she knew. Once more, she wasn't surprised. Pigafetta and Hans and Martin, fully formed inside her mind, sat in a circle. They laughed and they joked as she'd done in the first memory, and as they laughed, Pigafetta wrote. He recorded their story on the pages he held. And even though, just as in the earlier memory, Brodie couldn't read the shapes or squiggles that he made, she could hear the story they told. She knew he wrote in the language of Babel. And this time, without any doubt, she knew the story it told.

Back in the hotel room, Brodie sat down on the end of the bed. Her granddad moved to sit at her feet.

'This is a story,' said Brodie. 'A story of Avalon.'

'But I don't understand,' begged Hunter.

'Yes, you do,' said Brodie calmly. 'You don't need to understand the letter sounds or the shapes. You need to see the music of the patterns and the flow across the page.'

Sheldon was peering in. 'The music? On the page?'

'Look. It's here. It's in every line.'

He didn't look convinced.

'Remember how Elgar didn't really separate music and words?' she said. 'Do you remember how the two were combined? Well, look.' She was begging now. 'Look at the movement of the words. Look, Tusia, at the shapes, and, Hunter, look at the numbers and the spacing there in the pictures.' She flicked the pages. 'What's this story about?'

'We don't know,' blurted Tusia.

'But you do,' said Brodie. 'Look. We've always known. It's about a world where strange flowers bloom, where pools of renewing water flow and where the stars are bright. And there's a castle and linking islands. And in that place every voice is listened to and understood.'

Then, turning back to the front of the book, Brodie felt the meaning of the words and she began to tell a story. A story of a journey to Avalon. And the others listened.

She moved through the pages of MS 408 one by one. She stopped at the pictures of flowers and stars and she told their stories. It was easy to imagine how excited the three Knights of Neustria must have been by what they saw. It was easy to imagine the words they would have said. It was easy, because she allowed herself to become part of the storytelling circle she'd seen in her mind, like she'd done every day when she'd been a tiny child and stories had first been shared. When she came to pages where there were no pictures, she had to work harder, but she imagined the thrill and the excitement of the Knights as they discovered something new. And because she wasn't scared any more of getting it wrong, just like she'd been when she was tiny, the words came.

And the story of MS 408 was the story of Avalon. And they listened as she told it.

It was the story of three men who searched for a hidden island. It was the story of what they found and how they felt. It was all there in the language of MS 408. Every word of the story had always been there.

It had just taken till now for her to be brave enough, really strong enough, to read it.

And something happened as she told the tale.

The others in the room, one by one, took their seats on the floor. They sat in a circle, one next to the other, like an ancient tribe around a campfire.

And the story of Avalon spoke to them all.

And finally, everyone in the circle understood.

'Doesn't it seem like a cheat, somehow?'

They were sitting in the small garden of the hotel.

Just the four of them. Brodie and Hunter and Tusia and Sheldon. It was Hunter who'd spoken.

'I mean . . . Don't you think there should've been a code-book? That there should have been a dictionary and we should've been able to match the shapes from MS 408 with the words and make sense that way. That after all this time, it shouldn't have come down to just drawing on some sort of inner sense of what the words meant.'

Brodie shielded her eyes from the sun. 'If there'd been a code-book, someone else would have found it.'

'How d'you know?'

'The book's five hundred years old. And for one hundred of those years the very, very best minds in the world have been trying to make sense of what's written. If there'd been a code-book they'd have found it. If it had been a pattern formula they'd have found it. If it had been based on another world language they'd have found it. But no one ever did.'

'And it was really just that simple?' said Hunter.

Brodie scowled. 'Do you think what we did was *simple*?'

'I just mean, you know, easy?'

Her scowl deepened. 'The story was easy to read – eventually. But was it easy to get to that point? I don't think so! Think about what we've been

142

through! What we've faced! Who we've lost along the way.' She thought of her mother and Tandi then took a deep breath. 'None of that counts as easy. None of it.'

'But in the end, I mean. Reading MS 408. That part.'

'But without all the other stuff we couldn't have done it. Don't you get that?'

'Not really, B. I'm sorry.'

'We had to do all the work we did and face all the trials we faced and we had to spend so long with the manuscript that eventually, after all that, it sort of became part of us, and only then could we remember how to understand.'

'Seems kind of "deep" to me,' said Hunter.

'Yeah, well, *language* is complicated, isn't it? *Stories* are complicated. We had to go through everything we did before we could understand.'

'And how do you know that? I mean, all that clever stuff?' It was Sheldon's turn to ask her.

'Plato's cave,' she said.

'You'll have to give us more than that, B.'

'Smithies told me about it, at the very start. About how Plato told a story about people who were chained up in a cave and all they saw were shadows but they thought the shadows were real. Until one of them

143

escaped and got out in the real world and saw the world like it really was. Then, that person understood.'

'Understood everything?' asked Tusia.

'I don't think so. Just how things were not what they seemed.'

'And how does that fit with us, and MS 408?'

'I'm not really sure, but I just know that solving all the clues and the puzzles, and knowing what the Knights of Neustria were trying to protect and understanding how hard they fought to keep the secret, meant we knew enough, eventually, to be able to relax and read it. To get the story of the manuscript. To know what it was trying to say. And the language it spoke in was just a language we must all have known, deep down.'

'Sounds sort of spooky to me,' said Sheldon.

'I suppose. But is that any more spooky than knowing a land we thought existed only in myths and legends is actually real?'

'I guess not.' Sheldon took his harmonica from his pocket and began to play. It was quiet and mournful and perfect.

'That's a universal language,' said Brodie.

'You what?'

'The music. It speaks to all of us, doesn't it?'

'I suppose,' said Hunter as Sheldon played on.

'And no one tells you what the notes are. And you probably couldn't read them if they were written down. But that doesn't matter. You "understand" what the music is saying.'

'But some people write the music down though, don't they?' said Tusia.

'Of course. Musicians do. And the writing of MS 408 was a written language, the Patagonian giant Paul, the last to know it. But no one lives now who can write that way or read it. But we can understand it.'

'But we've got to hear the music, right?' said Hunter, pointing at Sheldon.

'I suppose. But you know, deaf people can "experience" music.'

'How?'

'They can feel it. Through the vibrations.'

'Yes. And we had to "feel" the language of MS 408. And we had to know that Pigafetta had been to Avalon and we had to know all about the Knights of Neustria. When we knew all that, then we had enough information to "hear" the words. To let them work with the pictures and for us to know what Pigafetta was trying to say.' She paused. 'We know enough now to hear what it says.'

Hunter sighed deeply. It was clear he was trying to drink in all Brodie had said and digest it. She could tell he wasn't quite sure. She could tell by watching him, his mathematical brain was trying to sort all the information and line it all up to make sense.

'It's like the beauty of a sunset,' said Tusia quietly.

Hunter turned to face her. 'What?'

'Or the complicated shape of snowflakes.'

Brodie didn't think it was possible for Hunter to look more confused.

'You can't break those things into pieces, can you? Not to understand them, I mean. You see the whole thing. The whole shape. And you *know*.'

'Know what?'

Tusia shook her head. 'Just something inside that can't be put into words. Something that doesn't need words.'

'So you're trying to say,' Hunter began nervously, 'MS 408 being written in a code beyond words isn't a cheat or a way out.'

'No,' said Brodie. 'Not a cheat or a way out. But the most perfect answer there could possibly be. The only real answer.' Understanding drummed like hail inside her mind. 'The answer to the code of MS 408 was never "out there". It was always somewhere inside us. And that's not cheating. That's just the way it is.'

Hunter's shoulders relaxed. His face became

unlined. And as she watched him, Sheldon continued to play. And the piece he played sounded like Elgar's music 'Nimrod'.

And there in the garden, without really knowing how, she realised she understood the music in the way it was meant to be understood. She understood the code.

'We should work out where we're going.' Smithies stood at the top of the steps to the garden. The sun was behind him and he looked younger than Brodie had seen him look before. A new energy surged inside him.

Brodie breathed in deeply and for just a moment Hunter caught her eye. She knew then he finally understood.

Tusia led the way back inside the hotel. They met, as they'd done so many times before, in Granddad's bedroom, crowded round his bed. This time three maps spread across the duvet. Pigafetta's unnamed lands; the nine islands of MS 408 and de Judicibus's map from the caves inside the Blue Ridge Mountains.

Tusia perched on the very end of the bed. 'I've been thinking about Helen Weaver,' she said.

'Have you?' laughed Hunter.

Brodie had to agree it was an odd thing to say.

'We always supposed she ran away from Elgar, didn't we?'

Sheldon looked confused. He'd missed this part of the code-cracking, but the idea of anyone running away from his favourite composer obviously caused him some distress.

'I mean, we thought Elgar must have told her about the search for Avalon, and all about the Knights of Neustria. And that was why she broke off the engagement and ran away.'

'Well, it was, wasn't it?' said Hunter. 'She did run off. Went to New Zealand and had two sons with another man and one of them was Van der Essen, the man who travelled with Voynich to find MS 408.'

'Yes. That's what we *thought*. But then I got to thinking that if her son was such an adventurer and so keen to track down Elgar and visit him and involve him in the writing of the Firebird Code, then perhaps Helen didn't really run *away*. Perhaps she ran *to*.'

'OK, Toots. Totally lost me now.'

Tusia was obviously trying to choose the words she would use to explain. 'I think now,' she said deliberately, 'that Helen Weaver left Elgar, not because she was scared of Avalon, but because she wanted to find it.'

'Really?'

'New Zealand,' Tusia said decisively. 'A Pacific Ocean island.' She pointed down at the maps. 'Doesn't that fit with all we've worked out?'

Brodie looked where she pointed.

'The place we're looking for has got to be somewhere in the Pacific Ocean,' added Tusia. 'That's where there's gaps in Pigafetta's explanations. That's the part of the story where he hid the folded page to give us details about the coded book. Avalon's in the Pacific Ocean. It must be. And I think Helen knew.'

'So d'you think she ever found it?' asked Sicknote.

Tusia shrugged. 'Not sure. It's not very likely because I guess most Europeans thought even if Avalon did exist, it wouldn't be so far away. But it fits now with what we know. And it fits with the maps we've got.'

Friedman lifted up de Judicibus's version. It showed a vast expanse of water and tiny flecks of land. 'So if this is the large-scale map of the islands in the ocean, then the other two maps show the detail of what we'll find.'

Brodie wanted to hug him. It was the way he said 'we'll find', as if there was absolutely no doubt now they would. That getting to Avalon was something which would actually happen now.

'But the Pacific Ocean's huge,' said Hunter. 'I don't

want to put a downer on things, but we have been over this. It's a quarter of the world's water. There're twenty thousand islands there. How on earth, or more importantly, how on sea, are we ever going to find it with a map from de Judicibus that's so vague?'

No one answered.

'We need some sort of marker. Some numbers. Some directions.'

He screwed his face up in concentration. He pressed his hands against his eyes. Then he breathed out.

He wore, then, the sort of look Brodie had seen him wear before. His eyes glinted like he'd heard some private joke and he was laughing at the punchline.

'What?' she said. 'What have you worked out?'

'It's a long shot, B.'

'It's a long ocean,' she said in return. 'We need all the shots at success we can get.'

'One six two seven five,' Hunter said.

Tusia groaned. 'What's he on about now?'

'Remember Shakespeare's memorial in Leicester Square in London. Where he held the scroll that said *There is no darkness but ignorance*? On the ground there were markers with distances. The statue was pointing. And directly in the line of his hand was this marker. We talked about it. If everything's connected, if all the clues are working together and the Knights of Neustria left us more signs, then maybe that marker's important.'

'You remember a distance from a marker on the ground which we saw months and months ago?' said Sheldon.

'Yes,' Hunter said defensively. 'Like B remembers stories and Toots remembers chess moves and you remember music notes. That's what *I* do.'

'OK,' said Sheldon apologetically. 'I get you. So this marker. It had that number, right?'

Hunter nodded. 'One six two seven five.'

'And why are you so sure that's important now?'

'Because it was the number of kilometres from the statue to a place in the Pacific Ocean,' explained Hunter.

Brodie felt her skin bristle with excitement. 'Which place?' she said.

'Fiji.'

Brodie knew she was scowling but she couldn't help herself. 'It's too big a leap. You said there's thousands of islands in the Pacific and now you're sure we should go to Fiji. It's too much of a risk.'

'It's a good idea,' said Granddad quietly.

'What?' cut in Sheldon. 'Now you're agreeing with him just because he remembers Shakespeare's hand was stretching in the direction of a plaque for Fiji.

How does that make sense?'

'Because we've got to start somewhere,' said Mr Bray. 'And because of the name.'

'The name?'

'Fiji. And what it means.'

'Go on,' pressed Brodie.

'Fiji means "Beautiful Island". To me that sounds like a good island to start on.'

'I agree,' said Tusia.

Brodie tried not to look too shocked. Hunter and Tusia so rarely agreed on anything. 'Why are you so sure he's right?'

'Oh, I'm not sure he's right at all,' Tusia explained. 'But I reckon it's about time we actually started physically searching for the place of Avalon.'

'So why d'you agree we should start by going there?' said Sheldon.

'My brothers. That's where they are. Both of them. In Fiji.' Brodie remembered Tusia had talked about that in their very first meeting all that time ago in Station X. 'They're doing environmental research,' she went on. 'And I can't think of any better plan than to start this whole attempt to find Avalon by going to see them.'

Brodie was sure the rest of the adults wouldn't agree.

They couldn't just pack up and travel to Fiji, surely?

But no one looked like they were going to say anything against the idea. After all, they were the same people who surely couldn't make sense of an ancient manuscript written entirely in code. And just look at what had happened there.

'They told me the Suppressors did terrible things,' Kitty said quietly. 'I didn't know about all *this* though.'

Kerrith put the file of papers on the table. Her breath was constricted. The information was overwhelming.

'It's gone on for centuries then?' said Kitty.

Kerrith nodded. 'Stories and histories rewritten. A new past as well as a new present given to the people. Anything that can affect the balance of power suppressed.'

Kitty reached to take two photographs from the top of the file. 'Team Veritas never really knew, though, exactly how it worked.'

'The Tyrannos Group are in charge,' explained Kerrith. 'Of all we read and see and learn.'

'And?'

'Stories that those in control didn't want to be heard were altered or filtered out. People were reeducated to learn new ways to see the world. Native stories were destroyed from the record.'

'But the history of real events?'

'Even more complicated,' said Kerrith. 'If stories slipped through the net, if mistakes were made, then it seems that other people have been employed to alter how the history books record what happens. See this photograph of Nikolai Yezhov,' she said, taking another image from the file.

'Here he is in a photograph with Stalin the Russian President. But then, he falls out of favour with Stalin and so Suppressors airbrush him from the photo.' The second photograph Kerrith took from the pile showed the same image but Stalin was now alone. The second man was missing from the shot.

'And here,' she went on. 'A picture of a group of people who helped Lenin when he was young. This man's Alexander Malchenko.' She pointed at a tall man in the left of the photograph. 'But see here how he's been erased from the photograph. History's been rewritten to show he wasn't there.'

Kitty looked down at the photographs she was holding. These, unlike the others, were modern snapshots, recently taken.

'The Director,' said Kerrith, leaning forward and pointing at a man smiling in the back line of the group scene. 'Taken at the meeting of the Tyrannos Group. And yet,' she pointed at the other photograph depicting the same scene but this time the man was missing, 'here he is, gone.'

'Vanished,' said Kitty, 'because he made a mistake and didn't bring down the team from Station X.'

'So do you understand what this means?' Kerrith asked quietly.

If Kitty did she wasn't willing to put her fears into words.

'It means the Suppressors control what's said and what's remembered. They have total power over how we see the stories of now and the stories of the past.' She flicked back to the centre of the file. A section on the Cultural Revolution in China in 1966. She scanned the pages again. 'It says here the people were told to destroy something called the "four olds".'

'The four what?'

'Four olds,' went on Kerrith. 'Old customs, old habits, old cultures and old ideas. Do you realise how big this makes the whole notion of suppression? Stories, ideas, all capable of being filtered and controlled. All this tampering and destruction is a never-ending job.'

'The team at Station X are on to this.' Kitty said slowly. 'They don't know everything you do, but they've worked out a lot of it. And they think they know where the document of MS 408 will take them. They think the manuscript talks about a place where everyone is treated equally.' She hesitated for a moment. 'The Suppressors would want to destroy that, wouldn't they? They'd want to wipe any trace of such a place from history.'

'Yes.'

Kitty thought for a moment.

'You've remembered something,' Kerrith pressed.

'Something important they wouldn't want those in the Black Chamber to know?' She could feel the excitement rising.

Kitty's lips were tight.

'You made me a promise,' Kerrith said firmly.

Kitty's hands were shaking as she opened her bag and pulled out notes and scribblings. She laid them across the table. 'I wrote down all I could. Made copies of their connections. I was scared when Summerfield was asking questions but I think there were things. Connections they made and never followed up.' A crumpled leaflet from Westminster Abbey fell to the floor. Kitty picked it up and smoothed it flat.

On the edge of the leaflet were tiny smudges of blood. And on the bottom, written untidily, was a number and the name of a place. 'Fiji. Is this important?'

'Maybe.'

# Sea Gypsies, Rapa Nui and the Land of Fire

Jurek and Kirill were waiting at Nadi airport.

The heat was overwhelming.

So was Tusia's welcome.

For nearly a month she, Smithies and Fabyan had been in charge of the arrangements. They'd done as much research as they could. Tried hard to be fully prepared. During everything, Tusia had been calm and contained.

Until she saw her brothers.

'Guess she's happy to see them,' said Hunter.

'She does seem quite pleased,' Brodie said awkwardly. She guessed Hunter was probably thinking about the lack of interest from his parents about them flying so far away. They had work, he'd explained, again.

Brodie herself was just glad to have landed.

Before arriving in New York a few months ago, she'd flown absolutely nowhere. Now it felt like she'd travelled round the world. In fact, she really had.

It should have felt wonderful to say she'd been to San Francisco and Sydney. Really, she'd only seen their airports. Still, the one in Australia was nice, even if the quarantine staff were particularly keen to check no one had smuggled food into the country, something Hunter found a little disturbing. He also found disturbing the amount of time they'd been travelling. 'Thirty-three and a half hours,' he said over and over again, as if by saying it the length would shrink somehow.

Ingham winced every time the length of the journey was mentioned. He straightened his flight socks and announced again he'd keep wearing them for the next three days just to make sure he hadn't developed a DVT.

The moaning stopped when they heard the music.

Three men stood in the arrivals lobby playing ukuleles and singing.

'Welcome to Fiji,' said Jurek, pointing to the musicians. 'You're going to like it here.'

Sheldon's grin showed that he at least was sure about that.

The boys' apartment was small and stuffy. They'd made up beds for everyone, explaining that anyone under twenty had a space with cushions and sheets on the floor. Kirill cooked supper and, although Brodie wasn't sure what it was, it tasted wonderful.

'Tomorrow,' said Jurek, 'you can finally tell us why you're here.'

Brodie hoped the brothers had set aside a good long while to listen.


Summerfield read the internal memo again. It was taking a while to sink in.

The latest papers from Site Three made confusing reading.

It was true he knew little of how the operation there worked. In the early days of his work with Kerrith, she'd kept him pretty well informed. That was when she still spoke to him. Those days had long gone. Now all communications were via memo.

This memo had four names on it. Only one caught his eye. Hantaywee Fabyan. He circled the name with his pen and then switched on his PC.

It may be nothing but he'd been trained to look for connections. This couldn't be a coincidence. Not after what he'd found in Kerrith's file, surely. It was time to let the Chairman know.

But there was something else he could do first. He'd got the authority to do it and it seemed a waste not to try.

He opened the department search engine and scanned the available icons. The cursor hovered over the one he needed. *PASSPORT USE NOTIFICATION*. He clicked it open and typed the name from the memo very carefully into the subject box and pressed 'enter'.


'We're looking for an island,' Tusia said at last, 'somewhere in the Pacific Ocean.'

Kirill did a very bad job of stifling a laugh. 'You know Fiji alone is made up of three hundred and thirty-two islands and there's about twenty thousand more out there floating around in all that sea.'

Tusia frowned. 'Yes, we know all about the size of the ocean.'

Jurek's eyebrows arched. 'Really? You *really* know all about the ocean and how vast it is?'

'Yes,' Tusia said defensively. 'Why?'

'Well, I sort of thought I knew about the size of the ocean when we came here, but truly, I didn't have a clue. It's all about the water here. Everything. The land and the islands are important but it's really all about the ocean.'

'How d'you mean?'

'Everything that happens here in the Pacific is linked to the water. It's so strange to be in a place where the land is really only just a little part of the story. D'you know, there are people who live in the Pacific who very rarely set foot on the land?'

'Where do they live then?'

'On the sea. In boats. They spend all their lives aboard. They're born there and maybe die there. They're called Bajau or Sea Gypsies and they adapt so well to life in the water, some even feel land-sick when they try to walk on dry ground.' Kirill sighed. 'So if you're looking for an island, then OK. But really, life in this part of the world is all about the sea.'

Tusia looked frustrated. 'Yeah, well. We are looking for an island. Quite an important island.'

'Does this island have a name?' said Jurek, passing round a plate of food which Hunter took rather eagerly.

Tusia flicked a glance in Smithies' direction. He nodded. 'The island's called Avalon,' she said.

It was odd how one word could change everything.

It all came out then, details tumbling one after another, about the encoded book and the hidden map and the pirate's sword. And all the clues and the puzzles and the Knights of Neustria who hid them. And with every extra detail the brothers looked more and more amazed.

'Are you absolutely sure?' said Jurek for about the fourth time, his eyes bulging.

'Yes,' insisted Tusia, and Brodie thought how wonderful it was that her own sureness had increased with the telling of the tale.

'But Avalon.' The way Jurek said the word made it sound as if he wasn't sure his mouth could really say it aloud. 'That's just a made-up place, right?'

Tusia squared up to her brother and Brodie could tell Jurek was a little nervous. In the years that had passed since he'd seen his sister, she'd grown in strength as well as size. 'It's real,' she said. 'Just like your sea gypsies. It doesn't sound as if it could be. But it is. And the issue is, somewhere in this enormous ocean you keep going on about, it's waiting to be rediscovered.'

'But if people knew, if people believed it was real, then wouldn't there be millions of people swarming there? I mean, didn't King Arthur go to Avalon to be "restored"? Aren't there magic swords and things in Avalon? If people knew . . .'

'People don't,' said Tusia. 'That's the point. It's been kept a secret for centuries and protected by code.'

'But you hope to find it?'

'And then what?' Jurek's face was creased in question.

Brodie looked away. They hadn't really thought that far.

'We're not sure,' said Hunter. 'But it's important we find it because there are others who are watching what we do and their plans for the island can't be good.'

And then they explained about the Suppressors and the race against time. And about Tandi.

The air felt heavy then, full of awkwardness pressing against them.

'We've got to find Avalon before the Suppressors do,' said Tusia, and this time she didn't look strong. She looked very fragile and Jurek reached out to hug her, obviously wanting to protect her and to make things right. And Brodie knew then, for the first time since they'd begun to explain, that the brothers believed them.

Kirill brought them drinks and more food and then lit the lamps in the darkening room. Then Tusia laid out the map from the Blue Ridge Mountains so her brothers could see.

'We've studied all the writings about Magellan's journey across the Pacific,' said Friedman. 'We've tried to make decisions about where Pigafetta could have landed, but really it could be anywhere.'

'Not exactly narrowed it down then, have you?' said Jurek.

Brodie felt embarrassed. It seemed stupid, now they were here, gazing down at a map that covered so many miles and just hoping somehow they'd stumble upon Avalon after all the careful clues and codes that had hidden everything else they knew. And then she remembered how the codes had hidden the location and how the words had been important. And it didn't feel stupid. It just felt like they would need to work hard.

'I've been thinking,' Sheldon said, nibbling on some pineapple. 'We probably just have to start at the beginning of Pigafetta's writings when the crews reached the Pacific Ocean. That's the only place to start.'

'Tierra del Fuego,' said Brodie quietly.

'Pardon?' said Mrs Smithies.

'Land of fire,' said Brodie. 'That was the first thing Pigafetta wrote about after they'd sailed through what's now called the Strait of Magellan and into the Pacific Ocean.' She loved the sound of the words in her head.

'Tierra del Fuego is part of South America,' said Tusia.

166

# Where is Avalon?

- Tierra del Fuego - 'Land of Fire'

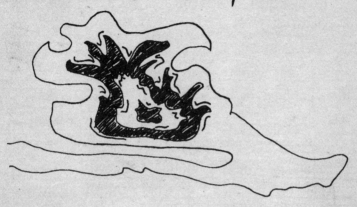

- 'Ring of Fire'

We'll get there Brodie

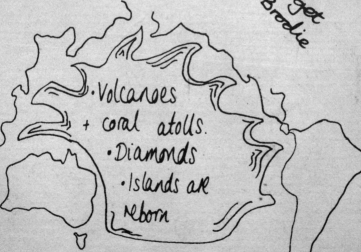

- Volcanoes
+ coral atolls.
- Diamonds
- Islands are reborn

'Yeah, well, maybe,' corrected Jurek.

'Why maybe?'

'Well, the thing is, so much of the land in the Pacific Ocean is "land of fire".'

Brodie knew it was hot, but she wasn't sure what Jurek meant.

'You must have heard of the Pacific ring of fire,' he said. Brodie wasn't sure she had but the words 'ring of fire' bubbled in her mind. 'Volcanoes,' Jurek said, helping himself to a slice of coconut. 'They're openings in the crust of the earth where fire and lava push through, forcing the surface of the earth into new shapes. The ring of fire stretches right round the edge of the Pacific Ocean. The islands you see in the Pacific are mostly volcanoes, or the remains of volcanoes where the fire has died and the coral has risen up from the sea. Coral atolls, they're called.'

Brodie couldn't help being reminded of phoenixes rising from the ashes.

'Most of the islands in the ocean are formed by the fire,' went on Jurek. 'Beautiful things are created by volcanoes. Diamonds even, did you know?'

Brodie did know. The jeweller at Tiffany's had told them as he'd shown them the boron diamond. So lands and precious things were made by fire. Avalon, then, rising from the fire like a phoenix somewhere in the Pacific Ocean. It was almost too beautiful and too brilliant to believe.

'And after the fire has formed the islands,' interrupted Kirill, 'they're given life by the wind.'

'What does that mean?' pressed Brodie.

'The coral rises up from the ocean and then the wind carries seeds and plants and sometimes even animals to the atolls and new life, and so new islands take shape.'

'It's brilliant,' said Brodie, feeling just a little bit light-headed. 'What you're saying is, the islands are born again from the ashes of the fire and then they rise up like towers of the wind.'

'She OK, your friend?' said Kirill, digging Tusia sharply in the ribs.

'Oh, yeah, she's fine. She's just all about the story, that's all.'

'That's all very nice,' Kirill said, 'but it doesn't help you find your island, does it?'

Brodie wasn't sure this was necessarily true. 'Story' had helped them find out nearly everything they knew so far.

Hantaywee blinked her eyes against the sun then squeezed Evie's hand. 'You'll be OK?' she said.

Miss Longman strode to take the older woman's

other hand. 'Of course she'll be all right. She's got us. It's you we're worried about.'

Hantaywee lowered her head. 'I can do this.'

'Don't you want it to be over?'

'It will be over soon. All of it.'

Mr Willer smiled at her. 'You're very brave.'

Hantaywee clutched at the piece of paper in her hand. 'I have to be.'


'So come on then,' said Kirill. 'If you're all about the story, where did the travellers go next as they worked across the ocean? What's next in the story?'

Brodie thought hard about all she'd read. 'Magellan talks about two small islands where there were no people, only birds and trees. He called these the "Isles of Misfortune". Where are they on this thing?'

Kirill looked down at the map. 'Great name, don't you think? Islands of Misfortune. Almost as good as the "Desolate Region".'

Brodie didn't think that place sounded very cheery either. 'Where's that?'

Kirill pointed to the map. 'It's this vast expanse of water here. There's little wind in this part of the ocean and so boats can drift along for days moving in no particular direction. You'd expect any islands you passed by there to be *islands of misfortune*, unless a north wind picked up and carried you.'

'A north wind?' confirmed Tusia.

Her brother looked up. 'Yeah. Why?'

'Oh, it's just I was climbing on the roof of this tower once,' Kirill didn't look at all surprised, 'and it was a Tower of the Winds. And the four winds should have been painted on it. Except on this tower there was only one. Borea. The North Wind.'

'And that reminded us of the story of Hyperborea, a place where people could live for ever and it linked in with the story of Avalon,' explained Brodie.

'You really are all about the stories, aren't you?' laughed Jurek.

'Well, that's how we made our links and our connections.'

'OK,' said Kirill, leaning back in the chair once more and this time lifting his hands behind his head. 'Make your connections now.'

Brodie looked confused. 'But we came here to get you to help us find Avalon.'

'But you're the ones with the know-how. Come on. Use the map. Make the connections you talked about.'

'He does this,' whispered Tusia. 'I should have warned you. Mum and Dad were always keen we worked things out for ourselves. It's just what they do. Push us to work things through.'

'OK,' said Brodie. 'The North Wind. Hyperborea. The clues from the Tower of the Winds. Supposing Magellan's crew were floating about around here in the Desolate Region and the North Wind began to carry them further up the ocean.' She dragged her hand across the map. 'Maybe we should start thinking about finding Avalon somewhere up here.'

'Seems a bit vague. Are you really sure someone didn't write down more clearly where they went?' Jurek said.

Brodie looked up from the map.

'Pigafetta did,' said Smithies. 'But we think he didn't write down everything, *that's* the point. We think he kept the location of Avalon a secret by missing out places some of the ships went to. Avalon must have been on an island only some of the ships went to.'

'It was a fleet of boats to begin with,' cut in Ingham. 'Five of them. Only one made it back. But during the time in the Pacific Ocean there were three of them. Maybe one of the ships split off and went away from the others and that's when Avalon was found.'

'How did they meet up again?' said Kirill. 'If these ships got separated? It's not like they had radio or computers back in the day, is it?'

'I read about that bit,' Hunter said. 'They put a

sign of a cross and rocks on the edge of the islands as a marker to show they'd been there. If one ship broke away from the others like we think, then it could have gone to Avalon and then sailed on.' His smile broadened. 'So I guess what we should be looking for if we want to find Avalon is an island with rocks on it as markers.'

The brothers looked across from one to the other. 'Really? You're looking for an island with rocks as markers?'

'I guess.'

'And you think that island will be Avalon?'

Hunter looked across at the rest of the team. 'Well, maybe.'

Jurek folded his arms. 'Job done then. I've found your Avalon.'

The air crackled with heat and excitement.

'If you're looking for an island in that part of the ocean, with rocks stacked up on it, then there's only one place it can be.'

'Well, go on then,' blurted Tusia.

'I reckon your Avalon is on Easter Island.'


'If you want impressive stone markers, then Easter Island is the place,' explained Jurek after he'd replenished the plates and everyone had settled

Where is Avalon?
Isle of Misfortune
Desolate Region
Ring of Fire
Easter Island and the Rapa Nui
Bird-man

down enough to hear.

'Can't get more impressive, in fact,' joined in Kirill.

'What the coconut milk are they on about now?' said Hunter. 'These two are even more bonkers than their sister,' he added in a quiet whisper before helping himself to another slice of pineapple.

Brodie tried to ignore him. 'In what way impressive?' she said.

Jurek spread his arms to explain. 'Well, there's these great big statues called Moai. They are shaped like warriors and they are spread around the edge of the island. There's over eight hundred of them and the Rapa Nui are very proud of them.'

'Hold on. I'm lost now. Rapa Nui. Who are they?'

'People led by the Bird Men.'

Brodie sank back on her heels.

'Hey, don't look at us like we're the nutty ones,' said Jurek. 'You're the ones who've flown here looking for a mythical island and all I'm saying is perhaps the Bird Men and the Moai fit the bill.'

Tusia stood up. Brodie loved watching her when she took charge. She had a steely determination which brought hush to the entire room. 'Slowly,' she said, 'tell us about these statues and the Bird Men.' She added the word 'please' as an afterthought but there was no way Jurek was going to argue with her anyway.

'The people of Rapa Nui built large stone monuments called Moai which they put all around the island's edge. That's what fitted with your idea about Avalon. The stone markers. Remember?' He carried on with his explanation. 'Each year they had a festival to choose a Bird Man for the island. Candidates were chosen to pick someone to go and collect the first sooty tern egg of the season from a nearby rock, and then swim back with it, to Easter Island. The islanders considered their Bird Men to be like gods.'

Brodie loved the story.

'Bird Men,' hissed Sheldon. 'D'you think there's a link to the phoenix?'

Brodie took a deep breath. Certainly swimming from an island out to a rock and back again would look like some sort of death and then rebirth, and she wanted more than anything for it all to be that simple. But the stories, as brilliant as they were, were getting muddled.

'We've got to slow this down,' she said.

'What?' said Kirill defensively. 'I've found your Avalon.'

'I'm not sure you have.'

Every eye in the room turned towards her.

'Oh, come on, B. It's worth a shot. Surely?'

'You don't have to dismiss it straight away,' said

Friedman, and his words hurt her.

'I want it to be this easy,' she snapped. 'Of course I do. But we've got to think this through. Listen to the story and fit it with what we know. And make sure we're not jumping to conclusions just because we're tired and we've come so far and we've tried for so long.'

Tusia looked offended, as if every word Brodie said was an insult to her brothers.

Brodie looked down at the map. 'OK. Easter Island. It's in the right sort of place. It's near the ring of fire and near the Desolate Region of the Pacific. And I love the story of the statues. But we've got to be careful.' She blinked hard, trying to make the problem clearer to see. 'We thought of Easter Island because we talked about Pigafetta stacking rocks on the shoreline but suddenly the rocks have become statues. Are you saying that after Pigafetta discovered Avalon he had time to knock up a few statues to put on the edge of the land? And over eight hundred of them? It doesn't make any sense.'

'But the Bird Men, B? What about the Bird Men?'

Brodie let the information wash over her. 'That bit I like.'

'You like the bit about the birds?' said Jurek.

'It's just we're kind of looking for links to

phoenixes,' said Sheldon quietly. 'It's all part of the links in the clues. That's why she likes it.'

Jurek's brow lined in concentration.

Brodie could feel the disappointment on the air. She could barely bring herself to look up. 'This Easter Island,' she said quietly. 'Do people live there?'

'Oh yeah,' said Kirill. 'Over four thousand of them. And there're visitors all the time to see the statues, of course.'

His words didn't have the impact he was hoping for.

'You don't want there to be people there?' he said.

'Well, if there's loads of people, looking round at the statues and things, wouldn't they have found the part of the island that's Avalon?' said Brodie tentatively. 'I mean, if the world knows about the Moai, wouldn't they know if the island was Avalon?'

Tusia linked her arm through her brother's. 'Hey. It was a good idea. Really. And we've found all the time, it's little things we say and tiny things we dismiss that eventually lead us to the answer.' She squeezed his arm. 'It's what code-cracking's all about.'

'So if that's true,' said Kirill, obviously trying not to look too crestfallen, 'what have we just dismissed that we should focus on?'

Brodie racked her brain. 'The phoenix link, perhaps,' she said.

'The fact the island's inhabited,' said Tusia.

'And the number of the statues,' said Hunter.

Jurek jotted down three words on a piece of paper.

# Phoenix

# uninhabited

# number

'So there's your answer,' he said.

Brodie took the piece of paper. 'That's our answer?'

'That's what you said.' He picked up the food plates and began to walk towards to the kitchen. 'You said it's the little things you dismiss which give you the answers. So there it is.'

Brodie didn't know what to say.

'Now, as our mum always used to say to us when we were worried, why don't you sleep on it?'

Brodie folded the paper over and mumbled the words again and again in her head.

The thought of sleep seemed overwhelming.

It took only minutes after her head hit the cushion for the world to drift away and sleep to come. But her hand clung tight to the piece of paper.

'It's too big.'

A heavy dose of jet-lag had woken Brodie at three thirty in the morning and she was sitting on the balcony of Jurek and Kirill's apartment, an atlas open at the page showing the Pacific Ocean propped on her knees, her finger tracing a dotted line down the centre of the map.

'What's too big? And where'd you find that?' said Hunter, pulling the screen door closed behind him and slumping down to sit beside her.

The air was heavy, thick with the promise of early morning sun. Brodie wasn't sure how anyone could ever get used to this heat. 'On the bookshelf,' she said. 'I couldn't sleep. You?'

Hunter raked his tussled hair. 'Not with Ingham's snores shaking the walls one side and your granddad's shaking the other. Don't know how Fingers and Toots manage to sleep through it.'

'Tusia sleeps through anything,' Brodie said.

'Yeah. Fingers too. Don't know how. Perhaps they don't think as much as me and you?'

Brodie shrugged. 'Maybe.' She looked down at the

map again. 'D'you think we'll ever really find it?'

It was Hunter's turn to shrug but then, quickly sensing this was the wrong response, he turned the movement into a twitch. 'Course we will. We do the impossible. That's what we do.'

Brodie tried to smile. 'But supposing what we've done is all we can. Supposing we've got as far as it's possible to go. Just knowing Avalon is there. Not actually getting there ourselves. That might be all we can manage.'

'Could be,' he said. 'But if we'd stuck to all that was expected we'd have not got as far as we have. Remember all we've been through. The caves, the tunnels, the nearly drowning.'

Brodie laughed. 'I know. And I have. But that was different.'

'Why?'

'Because then we were following clues. We were solving puzzles. *That* is what we do. And where's the puzzle now? It's just this.' She held the atlas out to him. 'The puzzle is, where, amongst all this sea, is land? The land we need. The land that's Avalon. That's the only puzzle. And I just don't know how we solve that.'

She leant her weight against Hunter's side and let the map book flutter in the breeze.

Hunter put his arm around her shoulder.

Stars flickered in the sky.

'It can't be all there is,' said Hunter quietly. 'Because if it is, then it's over.'

'Over?'

'All this. Veritas. The team.'

Brodie looked up. 'What will you do?'

She felt his body tighten. 'I suppose I'll go home and go back to school somewhere, if my parents still remember who I am.'

'Does it bother you?' Brodie said quietly.

'Bother me?'

'You know. Them not being involved. I have my granddad and Friedman. And Tusia has her brothers now. Even Sheldon's mum sends us a turkey at Christmas. You don't have anyone.'

'I thought I did,' he whispered.

Brodie swivelled round to face him.

'I've got the team, B. I've got all you lot, whatever happens, haven't I? Just because things change won't mean we're any different, will it?'

Brodie peered at him in the moonlight. And she remembered how much he'd disliked change when they first met.

'Wherever we are in the world, we'll still be part of Veritas, won't we? I mean, we may not use the name, but it will still be what we are. Part of the team.'

Brodie put her hand on his knee. 'Always. Wherever we are. Even if we don't use the name.'

They were silent then, as the edges of the atlas pages rippled up and down in the breeze.

'I don't want it to be over, Brodie,' he said.

She couldn't answer. Instead she looked down at the atlas and the world of water it showed.

Hunter put his hand on top of hers. 'Is it any help?' he said.

She wondered what he meant. Whether having him there was any help when she felt so desperate. And she wanted to tell him it was, but she didn't know how to say it.

'Jurek's list,' he said, opening her hand and taking the piece of paper she still held there.

Brodie shook herself. She felt her cheeks colour.

Hunter read the list aloud. '*Phoenix, uninhabited, number.*' He repeated the last word. 'That's my favourite,' he laughed.

'Number? Would never have guessed.'

'Maybe we're missing clues that've been left,' he said quietly. 'Maybe the Knights have narrowed our search down for us, but we're just not reading the clues.'

183

'OK. So, number. If that's a clue, what does it mean?'

Hunter thought for a while. 'I've got no idea. But . . . I did get to thinking we should remember one number we seem to have forgotten.'

'Really? Which one?'

'Nine,' he said. 'Yesterday, when we were talking to Jurek and Kirill, we kept going on about Avalon as if it's one island but it's not really, is it? Not if we think about Pigafetta's map in MS 408 and the book from the Beinecke.'

'I don't follow.'

'We made it sound yesterday like we're looking for one island, but we're really looking for nine.'

'OK,' said Brodie. 'Fair point. A group of nine islands fairly close to each other. We should have made that clear.'

Hunter seemed to be gaining energy. 'And if we go with the things we rejected then we've got to remember Easter Island was no good because it was inhabited. Which is why *uninhabited* is on our list.'

'Yeah. OK. A group of nine islands that are uninhabited, higher than the Desolate Region. I get all that, but it's still too big. There are thousands of islands in this ocean. That's the point.'

Hunter took the atlas on to his own lap. Brodie

could see from his face he was as frustrated as her as he peered at the specks of brown which marked land. 'How d'we find a group of nine amongst all these?' he groaned.

Brodie peered in close. The stars flickered overhead.

And then she saw something which made her stomach tighten.

There was a group of islands. Near the dotted line which sliced the page. She counted them quickly with her finger. Eight, not nine, but to the north of Easter Island. And by the small marks on the page was a symbol. A tiny star. There were lots of shapes and symbols across the map. But by this group, this knot of eight islands, there was a star.

She scoured the rest of the map. 'That star,' she yelped. 'What does that star mean?'

'Oh, here we go. You and your star connections. Are we back to the phoenix constellation yet again?'

Brodie grabbed the map. 'It's a symbol. And this key here,' she added, jabbing at the map, 'says it means the name's recorded somewhere else because it must have changed some time. 'Like "B" and "Toots" and "Fingers" . . . and "Firebird". All new names for old things.' She flicked to the next page. A list of names for some of the smaller islands were arranged alphabetically down the page. Brodie looked for the star symbol. Then her heart rose.

'We've got to tell the others.'

'We don't know for sure,' said Hunter, grabbing her as she pulled to stand. 'There's only eight islands. We could be wrong.'

Brodie spun round to face him. The moonlight made his face glow. 'And we could be right,' she said, choking back her words. 'We could be in the middle of the Pacific Ocean looking down at a map and we could be right. We could have solved the clues because it was the most important clue we ever had. From the very, very beginning when we first began, it was always about this clue.'

'I know. I know. But—'

'The very first code, Hunter! The very first step we took in this adventure. What was it called?'

'The Firebird Code.'

'So there's only eight islands and not nine. But it just has to be. You know it and I know it.' She rocked back her head and looked up at the sky. 'Even the stars know it.'

'OK. OK.' He held her by the shoulders. Then he took a breath and squared his shoulders. 'We tell them.'

Brodie bent down and hugged the atlas against her. She thought for a second she might burst until she'd said the words aloud. 'This time we really have found Avalon.'

# 8

# Beneath the Islands of Rawaki

The airport concourse had been rather busy, but the VIP lounge was less crowded. Kerrith put her case down and passed the file to the Chairman.

'You found it interesting reading?' he asked, swilling his drink in the bottom of the glass.

'Very,' she said. Her pulse was racing. She wasn't totally sure the logistics of her planning would work. She couldn't believe Summerfield had made the same connection to Fiji that she had. Kitty had noticed he'd kept the photograph of Leicester Square after the interview session. Summerfield must have noted the mile marker on the ground. Known Fiji was important. He'd made sure the Chairman knew about the connections.

'It's good your education's been extended,' the

Chairman said. 'I wouldn't want you to be unclear about what you're involved in.' He took a glug of the drink. 'And Miss McCloud.' He turned to look at Kitty. 'I'm of the belief that this information cannot be shared too soon with those who join us. Helps us all know where we are.'

Kitty fiddled nervously with the edge of her passport.

'So,' said the Chairman, downing the rest of his drink. 'You're both ready?'

Kerrith wasn't really sure whether this was a question or a statement.

'Must say that those oddballs from Station X have run us a right merry dance over the last two years. But seems the end must be in sight soon.'

Kerrith, too, was sure the end was coming.

As they walked towards the boarding gate she glanced one last time around Departures. She couldn't help but wonder how many other people might be taking flights today.


If felt like it had on the evening long ago when they'd crowded into the music room at Station X to listen to the music of the Firebird Box. There were new faces now. Mrs Smithies, Sheldon, Kirill and Jurek. But there was someone missing. Tandi.

Brodie tried not to think about her as they huddled in the rising heat of early morning, the faces all around her confused and expectant. She tried only to get her words in order so what she said made sense.

She failed.

'Rawaki? What does that mean?' Ingham shuffled forward and reached for the map. 'Rawaki, you say.'

Sheldon fiddled with his harmonica and leant over Ingham's shoulders as Brodie prodded at the map. 'Part of this group of islands here?' he asked. 'These eight?'

'I know. I know. There should be nine,' she said. 'But surely eight is close enough.'

Hunter began to mumble. 'Really depends on what context you're working in. The gap between two digits, when broken down into decimal parts, can be quite large when considered on some scales.'

'You're supposed to be on my side,' growled Brodie, seeing the expectation around the room had shifted now into definite confusion.

'I am, B. I am. Right beside you.'

'But there's only eight islands,' Ingham said again. 'I thought we were looking for a group of nine. The maps from Pigafetta suggest there are nine.'

'There are more maps?' said Jurek. 'You didn't say there were more maps.'

Brodie rubbed her forehead. 'I know. I know. What we showed you first was the map from de Judicibus which helped us know Avalon must be in the Pacific Ocean somewhere. But what we didn't show you were the two maps Pigafetta made.'

Tusia obliged and rummaged in the bags and cases they'd brought and pulled out the other two maps. 'One was from the coded document MS 408,' she said to her brothers, showing the map with the connecting islands, 'and this one is from the book Pigafetta wrote after he got home. He doesn't name any of the islands. But he draws nine though, see.'

'And it was the name that was important,' said Brodie, turning back to the atlas. 'That and where the islands are.'

'Where they are?' repeated Friedman. 'Looks to me as if they're in the middle of a very big ocean.'

Brodie took the atlas from Sheldon and flattened the page. 'The International Date Line, look. It runs right by the island of Rawaki. It's here sailors literally lose a day when they are travelling. It was the sailors who went with Pigafetta who realised there'd need to be a date line. That if you travelled from one side of the world to the other, you'd lose a day.'

She looked down at her two wristwatches. She knew better than anyone, time was man-made and it was possible to play all sorts of tricks with how it was measured.

'If you were going to make omissions in the record you kept of a journey, where better to miss things out than around this line? It would help explain why some of the entries don't tally between Pigafetta's writings and the pilot's. And if days can be lost here, then so can visits to Avalon. What d'you think?'

It was true the fog of confusion was thinning a little.

'OK. So say we ignore the fact there are only eight islands and we focus on the fact the islands are near the International Date Line. Why else should we be sure these islands, of all the thousands in the ocean, are the most likely to be where Avalon is?' said Tusia. 'What else have you got?'

'The name,' said Brodie.

'Rawaki?' said Ingham again.

'No. The group name for the islands,' Brodie said. 'According to the atlas the islands changed their name in 1979.'

'So what were the islands called before?' Mrs Smithies said, holding her husband tightly by the hand.

'The *Phoenix* Islands.'

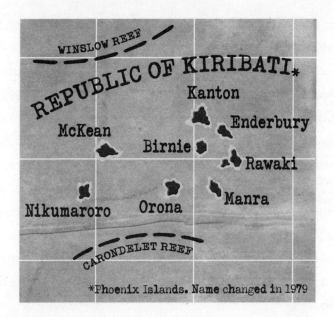

WINSLOW REEF

REPUBLIC OF KIRIBATI*

Kanton

Enderbury

McKean

Birnie

Rawaki

Nikumaroro   Orona   Manra

CARONDELET REEF

*Phoenix Islands. Name changed in 1979

'Five days? It takes five days? You've got to be joking.'

Kirill and Jurek had returned from their trip into Suva where they'd tried to arrange transport for the team to the Phoenix Islands. They didn't look happy. 'Five days by boat and that's if we can get you one to hire.'

Fabyan put down the bowl of breakfast fruit he was eating. 'Then we fly.'

'No one flies to Rawaki. They're uninhabited islands. There are no airports.'

'No,' said Fabyan, shuffling the papers he and Hunter had been poring over. 'You're right. But you're also wrong.'

193

Jurek frowned.

'According to all we've read, Kanton is one of the islands. And Kanton has an abandoned airstrip which was used by the Americans many years ago. I suggest that's where we start. And I suggest we fly there.'

Kirill's laugh was as loud as his sister's. 'Fly there. OK.' He folded his arms. 'That might be possible, I suppose, if you had access to a private plane and billions of pounds to pay for it.'

Fabyan stood up and tightened the drawstring on his crisp stripy pyjamas. 'Good job we have then,' he said.

There were musicians again at Nadi airport. Sheldon went closer to listen while Fabyan sorted out the paperwork at a private desk. Brodie sat on her suitcase and fanned herself in the heat. It was so weird to think they were leaving so quickly. Even weirder to think they had somewhere to go.

'You think she'll ever stop crying?' said Hunter, leaning over to whisper.

Brodie looked at Tusia, who was clinging rather tightly to her brothers. 'Doesn't look much like it.'

Brodie wiped a trickle of sweat from her neck. Watching Tusia sob, and knowing she'd probably cry throughout the flight, made her wish the brothers had agreed to come too. She looked up to the desk where Fabyan was busy filling in forms and passing what looked like a rather large wad of notes to the woman behind the desk. 'Ready then?' he said, balancing his wallet precariously on a stack of their checked passports. 'We've only got five minutes and unless we fly now, then we've no chance of getting to Kanton before the weekend. There's a storm brewing,' he added as explanation.

Brodie reached for her case. She didn't know that by the time she grasped the handle and stood again, things had shifted in her world and a die rolled that would raise the stakes.

Brodie had often read the expression that 'colour drained from someone's face'. She hadn't really ever seen it happen. Until now.

Fabyan turned grey. He looked so uncomfortable, Brodie was sure he was ill. He staggered forward and his eyes locked on somewhere far away.

Ingham was first to react. He steadied Fabyan and grabbed his arm. But Fabyan pulled free. He dropped his wallet, and coins and notes fluttered and rattled to the floor. A fan of photographs slid from the wallet and flapped on the polished tiles.

Fabyan walked forward. His eyes were unblinking.

And his voice, when it came, uttered a word Brodie and no one around her understood.

'What d'you mean, it's the same woman?' hissed Brodie.

Tusia, who'd forgotten temporarily about her crying, held the fallen photographs. 'Look. It's her. From his wallet.'

Brodie wasn't sure. The woman in the photograph looked young and full of life, this woman old and tired. 'Why's she here, in Fiji? And why won't he put her down?'

Fabyan had made his way through the group and was clinging now, much as Tusia had done to her brothers, to a tall but frail-looking woman with wide jet eyes and hair as dark as a raven's wing.

'I don't understand.'

It was obvious no one else did either.

'Excuse me.' The assistant from the check-in desk was growing anxious. 'We really need to clear this flight right now,' she said, her voice several tones higher than it had been before. 'We've got to clear the runway. This flight is not part of the schedule. We really need to—'

Friedman took the hint. 'Fabyan, mate, we've got to make a move. Are you OK?'

When Fabyan turned, Brodie could see he'd been crying. 'I thought she'd left me. I thought she'd gone.'

'Mate?'

Fabyan blew out a breath and wiped his face. 'I'm sorry. I'm sorry. Everyone, this is my wife.' He blew out a breath again, making it look like the words were mixing with the air and making it hard to breathe. 'Three years ago she vanished. I thought she'd given up on married life. Had enough of my collecting, and my ways. Enough of me.' The woman beside him patted his arm. 'But it seems I was wrong.' He drew strength from her but he could still barely form the words he needed. 'But she hadn't left at all. She'd been taken.'

Friedman stepped in closer. He swallowed deeply, drinking in what he'd heard. 'You? That place? You were there?'

'What does he mean, that place?' said Hunter.

'Is anyone else following this?'

But Brodie knew. She let go of the case and it rocked backwards and forwards on the floor. She moved to stand beside Friedman. 'Dad?'

'In one of their centres, Brodie,' Friedman mumbled. 'She was locked away.'

'It's OK. It's OK.'

The woman spoke then. She used the strongest

voice of them all. 'It's not OK. The Suppressors took me and they held me as their prisoner.'

'But how did you get away? How did you find us?' Tusia was speaking, her questions tumbling over one another.

The woman shook her head. 'None of that matters. It only matters that if I've found you, so can they. And they are coming.'

As the plane lifted from the ground, soaring over the crystal waters of the Pacific and the white sands of Fiji, Brodie pressed her palm against the window.

The last few moments on the ground had been frantic. Everyone had an opinion. No one could make a decision. Until Fabyan made it for them.

They'd go without him.

The rest of Team Veritas bundled on to the plane, scrabbling for seats, as Kirill and Jurek steered Fabyan and his wife away. It was better like this. If the Suppressors were close, someone needed to stay behind to try and fend them off. Time was running out. Whatever happened, as many of the team as possible had to make it to the Phoenix Islands.

'I'm scared.'

Hunter turned in his seat. 'We're all scared, B.'

'Not about the Suppressors,' she said, letting her hand slide from the window. 'I mean, I *am* scared about them, but I'm scared too about all this ocean. And about the islands and what we'll find there. And how we'll know what to do. And—'

'Whoa up there. Steady on, B.' He was trying to make himself look authoritative. Brodie could tell. 'We take this a step at a time. Like we always do. Just one step after another.'

'But what will we do when we get to Kanton? I mean, we've got no plan.'

'We'll wait and see what the caretakers suggest.'

'Caretakers?' said Brodie. 'I thought the islands were uninhabited.'

Hunter took a crumpled page from his pocket. The page he'd been reading with Fabyan back at the apartment. 'The Phoenix Islands *are* uninhabited. Except for Kanton.' He showed her the page. 'There are a group of about forty people who live there. They look after the island.' He moved his lips like the information was something to chew on. Then he passed the piece of paper to her. 'When we arrive, we can ask them what they know.'

Brodie looked down. On the paper was a sketch of the island, and the national flag of Kiribati, the government who had control of the islands. The flag showed a bird flying high above a setting red sun.

The sands of the island were pearl white, a thin ribbon against the blue. The water which lapped against them was so clear it was possible to see fish swimming and coral waving like branches in the breeze. The plane scudded up a cloud of dust as it landed and for a while it was difficult to see.

When the air stilled, the pilot opened the door and lowered the steps.

A gaggle of about thirty people surged forward when the engines cut. The pilot laughed and opened the hatch, unloading the food Fabyan had agreed could be flown over as part of the deal for giving the flight air clearance. 'Don't get many deliveries out here,' said Smithies, 'but you'd know more than most, the way to a person's heart is via their stomach, Hunter. Give a hand with the load.'

And so, in a melee of cases and boxes, the team followed the crowd to a large long building on the edge of the shore.

When the plane was unpacked and the pilot had said his goodbyes he restarted the engine. Brodie felt a pang of fear. But there wasn't time to doubt.

As the plane lifted from the airstrip, marking tracks in a clear blue sky, one of the islanders moved to stand beside her.

It was difficult to tell how old he was. His skin was cracked with age but his eyes looked young. He wore Western clothes but his feet were bare, his toes curling in the sand. 'My name is Kahuna,' he said after a while. 'In your language it means "hidden secret".'

Brodie felt her heart flap like the wings of a tiny bird.

'I'm a caretaker of the islands. But you have words for that in your language too.'

# Kahuna's Promise

Team Veritas sat around a campfire on the beach. The wood crackled as the flames escaped from inside.

Kahuna looked out to sea. He was perfectly still.

'Are you a Knight of Neustria?' said Smithies.

There was a spark of recognition.

'So you know why we're here?'

'I can guess.'

'So will you show us then? Take us to the place we came to find?' pressed on Smithies.

There was no answer.

'We came to find Avalon. We believe we're very close. Will you help us?'

Kahuna kicked sand towards the fire and it guttered a little and the flames weakened. 'No.'

\* \* \*

'All this way and the guy's not gonna let us get near,' groaned Hunter.

'You can't blame him,' said Tusia. 'He doesn't know us. Can't be sure we can be trusted.'

They'd been shown to small huts lining the edge of the beach. The adults had gone off to bed, but it was too hot to sleep. The four of them sat on the steps of the hut watching the dying embers of the fire.

'We've got to persuade him. Convince him it's safe,' said Tusia.

'How?' pressed Brodie.

Tusia shrugged. 'The others said wait until morning.'

'And when has being cautious helped us before?' asked Sheldon. 'We can't wait to persuade him. I reckon we should let the Knights do it.'

Sheldon led the four of them along the beach. Kahuna was sitting beside the dying embers of the fire.

The old man looked up and Sheldon curled his toes into the sand. 'We understand,' he said. 'We know why you won't show us. But we wanted you to see some stuff.' The sentence didn't sound as good as it had in their practice, but Hunter patted him on the shoulder encouraging him to go on. 'We've been following the clues of the Knights for years now. And we've found things.' He gestured to Tusia, who took the Coleridge ring and held it out. Hunter put down the sword and the blade shone in the final sparks of the fire. Then Brodie reached up and unfastened her locket. She put it on the sand beside the sword. 'We know that Pigafetta and Hans and Martin found Avalon,' he said. 'And we want to find it too.'

'Impressive,' Kahuna said. 'But I made a promise. You can't expect me to break it.'

'But we're on the same side,' said Tusia.

'So you know there are sides. And you know there are those who'd do Avalon harm.'

'We know all about that.'

The old man considered for a while. 'So you know that whatever you tell me, whatever you show me, however hard you beg, my answer will be the same.'

'But we just want to complete the journey we've made,' Brodie blurted.

'Completion is important to you?'

'Yes.'

Kahuna thought again for a moment and the wood in the fire crumbled into ash. 'I'm sorry. The answer is still no.'

'We tried, B,' Hunter said gently. 'Tomorrow we'll try again. Smithies will think of something.' He didn't even sound convinced of this himself. 'In the morning things will feel better.'

Brodie bit her lip. How could things possibly be better in the morning? They'd come this far. Avalon was just around the corner and some guy who'd made an ancient promise was making things impossible. The team was all about solving things that nobody else could. But how did they solve this?

She said none of this to Hunter and watched as he and Sheldon made their way inside the hut. 'I'll be in in a moment,' she said to Tusia. 'Seriously, you get some sleep. I'll be fine.'

But she wasn't fine. She was angry. Kahuna hadn't listened. He didn't understand. All they'd done and all the sacrifices they'd made to get this far.

She reached up to take her locket in her hand.

It wasn't there.

Her stomach plummeted. She'd had it moments before. It was part of what they'd shown him to try and make him understand. That and the sword and the ring.

She must have left it on the sand.

She raced back along the shoreline. The fire was completely dead now. The only light came from the moon and the stars. And the glint of the locket as it moved backwards and forwards, swinging from Kahuna's grasp.

She could barely speak to him. 'It was my mum's,' she blurted. 'And I made a promise too, you know.'

The old man looked confused.

'Open it,' Brodie urged.

Kahuna stilled the locket's swinging and clicked it open.

'My mum drew that castle. It's from Pigafetta's manuscript. And I promised myself I'd find it for her. Because she died trying to.'

The only sound was the wash of the waves against the sand.

Kahuna pressed the locket shut. He held it towards Brodie. 'I hear what you're saying. And I can tell you've paid a price for this search.'

'My friend died too. Only months ago. Isn't that

enough to show you we can be trusted?'

'But supposing it's not just about trust. Suppose it's about me being sure you know what's involved?'

'We came all this way. We solved all the clues.'

Kahuna held up his hand. 'I understand. But do *you* understand that if I show you the final steps of the journey, then completion comes at a cost?'

Brodie gripped tightly to the locket.

'Knights of Neustria make a promise too, Brodie. To protect Avalon whatever the cost. Supposing I let you go on from here, there can be no turning back. Can you make the Knights' promise that the needs of Avalon will come before anything else? Because I need you to be totally and completely sure?'

Brodie swallowed hard. 'I'm sure,' she said.


Kitty peered out of the aeroplane window. 'You know they were my friends,' she said quietly. 'For a while I was one of them. That felt good.'

'But you must have known all the time what you were there to do,' said Kerrith.

'I knew,' said Kitty. 'But there were days when I could forget. You know, they really were the oddest group of people I'd ever met. Some of them were so crazy, you'd cross the road if you saw them.'

Kerrith turned to face her.

'Sicknote, for a start. I mean, he looked weird. And he *was* weird.'

'Years of not being believed can do that to you.'

'And then Friedman. He was totally damaged.'

Kerrith remembered who'd caused the damage. She closed her eyes for a moment but all she saw behind her eyelids was the fire and the lighthouse and the man hanging from the light.

'Why did the Chamber torture him and not just kill him?' Kitty asked.

Kerrith considered her answer. She supposed it fitted with all the rest of the work the Tyrannos Group ordered in the name of suppression. 'There are worse things than death, Kitty,' she said. 'I suppose we thought, if we took Friedman from the group it would weaken their resolve.'

'It didn't do that though, did it?'

'No.' Kerrith hesitated. 'But then I suppose we thought, if the team knew the truth about what he'd done to Brodie's mother, they'd have to turn against him.'

'And that didn't work either. You see, they had this thing about truth. They didn't let go of things till they understood that.'

'I know that now.'

'But you thought you'd done enough?'

'We thought if we sent him back damaged they'd find the wounded man so distasteful they'd give up the fight altogether.' Kerrith looked down into the glass of drink she was holding as if a better way to share the answer would rise to the surface for her to take. 'If anything, though, it strengthened them. They saw what we'd done and it made the fight more real and them more determined to win.'

Kitty turned again towards the window. 'The kids were so nice to me,' she said.

'Yeah, well, maybe they weren't damaged.'

Kitty looked surprised. 'Oh, they were.'

Now it was Kerrith's turn for surprise. 'But they're talented and special. All of them.'

'That's why they're damaged. Their skills marked them out as different and that was hard for them. None of them fitted in anywhere else. That's why it's so difficult to realise I let them down.' She shuffled in her seat. 'Why did the Suppressors have to do what they did to Tandi?'

'Because it was ordered,' said Kerrith. 'And in the Black Chamber orders are carried out.'

'And that's why we're flying halfway round the world on the tail of the Team Veritas? To follow orders?'

'We're doing what we've got to do.'

'I just don't understand how the Chamber knows where they're going.' Kitty rested her head against the window and stared vacantly at the streak of clouds. 'I mean, without me there feeding back information.'

Kerrith took a deep breath. 'You gave us a way into the heart of the operation, Kitty. But the Chamber watches everything. Veritas leaves a trail behind it wherever it goes. Truth always does. And I suppose, now they know we're on to them, they've only been worrying about getting answers. Hiding their tracks was never enough of a priority for them.'

'And what we plan to do is the right thing?' said Kitty.

Kerrith looked once more into the bottom of her glass. 'It's up to you to decide,' she said.

The younger woman stared out at the sky and the taut light of a sinking orange sun.

Brodie sat by the side of the shore. She pressed her palms deep into the burning sand. Every now and then a wave washed in. The water didn't cool her skin. Heat raged from a place inside her.

The others were helping unload more food from a supply plane which had just arrived. The islanders lived on fish and coconuts but the plane brought rice and maize when those in the government of Kiribati remembered.

A shadow slid across her body. 'I bring chocolate,' a voice said from above her.

Brodie shielded her eyes and looked up.

'They've finished unloading and you look like you could do with cheering up.' Hunter broke a square from the end of the bar. The chocolate smudged around the edges as he passed it. 'Have to down it quick before it melts.'

Brodie licked her fingers. 'Thanks.'

'You OK, B? Because it's all sorted now. I don't know what was said but somehow the old guy's come round. He's going to let us go from here and find Avalon. It's all good.'

Brodie hadn't told anyone about her final discussion with Kahuna.

Hunter sat down beside her and lay back in the sand. 'Totally fabulous here, don't you think? I could get used to this and that's without even finding out which island Avalon's on.'

Brodie didn't answer.

'You don't like it?' he asked, sitting up and shaking sand from his shoulders.

'No. It's just . . .'

'You don't need to worry, now. Seriously, B. We're

nearly at the end.'

She couldn't tell him that was the part which worried her. 'Do you remember the Royal Pavilion?' she said.

'Of course. Why?'

'And how we found the box and the scarlet feather and then how the Suppressors were after us?'

'Yes, I remember,' he laughed. 'I can hardly forget us dangling on a rope and my not so impressive landing.'

Brodie winced. 'Tandi was there,' she said.

Hunter's eyes darkened.

'And you were injured. But I had to go on, alone. You remember?'

'What is this, B? You're not alone now. We're part of a team. But you're kind of scaring me.'

'I know,' she said, trying to force her mouth into something like a smile. 'But you remember that even as a part of a team I had to promise Tandi I'd do everything I could to keep the Firebird Box safe?'

'It was what you had to do, B.'

Brodie turned and looked towards the sea.

'So why the reminder of the sad story?'

She couldn't tell him what she knew because she didn't understand it herself. And she'd no idea what it would mean. 'Not every story has a happy ending,' she said quietly.

'You don't want to go eat with the others?' Kahuna sat down beside Brodie on the sand. The sun was setting, leaking its colours into the vast expanse of blue.

Brodie shook her head.

A breeze lifted. A single feather blew against her arm. Kahuna reached down and picked it up. He ran his finger along the shaft. 'Earthbound,' he said.

Brodie didn't know what he was talking about. He sat down in the sand beside her. 'This feather is from a bird that can't fly. The Phoenix Islands now have many of them. Their purpose to be here amongst all this ocean and never to take wing. Sad, don't you think? To never do what life has intended all along for you to do.'

Brodie wasn't sure how to answer him. She took the feather. It was scarlet. Like the feather in the Royal Pavilion when they'd looked so hard for the Firebird Code. A single feather that was to change everything and to show the answer was nearly found. She held the feather tight.

'You make a good team,' said Kahuna. 'A little odd, some of you, but a good team. We always wondered who it would be who'd find us. In my generation of guarding there have not been others. No one we could believe was here to do what needed to be done.'

'What will that be?'

'It's not my place to tell you. But Avalon will ask something of you.'

'And my promise means I'll have to do whatever I'm asked?'

Kahuna nodded. 'It's the Knights' promise.' He waited for a moment. 'Would you have come if you'd known?'

Brodie thought of all the puzzles and the clues and all that had been done to keep the story of Avalon safe. 'How can I tell if I don't know what I'll be expected to do?'

'It will be your chance to add to the story.' Kahuna stretched his finger and drew in the sand. 'It will be about completing a circle,' he said, connecting the beginning of the loop he'd drawn with the end.

'Do I have to be the one to complete the circle though?' said Brodie. 'Couldn't it be anyone?'

Kahuna retraced the sand picture with his finger. 'Who else would you want it to be? If there was a price to be paid, who would you rather had the task?'

Brodie didn't answer.

The old man stood up. His feet sank down in the

sand. 'We will lend you a boat,' he said. 'When will you leave?'

'Tomorrow?' She hesitated. 'I don't even know which of the islands we are making for.'

'You should be able to work it out,' Kahuna said.

Again, Brodie had no idea what he meant.

'The island you need is called McKean,' he said at last. 'But it hasn't always had that name.'

'What was it called before then?'

Kahuna answered as he walked away. 'The island was called Arthur.'


'McKean,' said Friedman, stretching one of the Knights' maps across the table. 'Why McKean?'

'Because it's changed its name,' said Brodie.

Everyone was waiting.

'It used to be called Arthur.'

'Perfect,' said Tusia. '*Of course* that's where Avalon is. Arthur Island. One of the Phoenix Islands chain.'

Hunter was smiling but Brodie knew that look. 'It sounds great and everything,' he said. 'And I get the name links and I don't want to put a downer on everything, and I hate to mention it . . .'

'Spit it out, boy.' Sicknote was struggling with the heat and any patience he'd had was thinning.

'It's just I'm still bothered by the number nine.'

Tusia rolled her eyes. 'Arthur Island. Phoenix chain. A Knight of Neustria here to check we can go ahead. How can you *possibly* be worrying about the numbers?'

'It's just both maps had nine islands,' Hunter said apologetically. 'I just think if there were nine on the map there should be nine islands in this chain. And there aren't. There's only eight.'

Kahuna moved forward and gestured to his own map. 'He's right. There are only eight islands. But if you look closely at the chain you'll see what you're missing.'

Hunter peered in. 'Are they two islands nearly touching?' he said, squinting slightly.

Kahuna nodded. 'Yes. And they are almost connected by a walkway of coral. No one bothered to name this as an extra island. But it is. The caretakers have to oversee a *total of nine* places. Does this help?'

Hunter's face relaxed into a smile. 'It more than helps.'

Tusia pushed her way to the front. 'So that really is perfect then. Two islands connected by hidden coral. Coral hidden *inside* the water.'

'Oh, here we go,' said Sheldon. 'Off on one of her rambles. What's she talking about?'

Tusia scowled but Brodie couldn't help feeling she was actually a little flattered. 'With every clue we've solved, the answer's been hidden. A secret. Something hidden under the surface.' She pulled herself up tall. 'If Avalon's really as important as we think it is, then part of the clue to finding it would be hidden. Part of the nine, but not on the surface.'

'And so what can you tell us about Arthur Island?' said Smithies.

Kahuna rubbed his chin, considering how to start. 'The island is small and heart-shaped. A large lagoon spreads across it. The land is home on the surface to many birds. But what you seek is inside the lava tunnels and chambers. The lava is ever changing and moving. The layout of the land shifting and growing. Avalon won't be visible to those who don't look with care. Planes can fly above and not see the openings to the chambers. The ground is uncharted and unmapped. A secret inside a secret.'

'And there's no one on the island?' said Mrs Smithies.

'Not in the parts the world sees.'

'But in the chambers?'

'There are the workers of Avalon,' said Kahuna, 'as there always have been.'

'And is there anything we should know?' said

Ingham. 'Before we go?'

Kahuna's face darkened. Brodie wondered if the others saw. 'I think all is known that has to be.'

# 10

# St Elmo's Fire

They left Kanton at night.

There was a storm coming. The islanders could tell. The air was changing. There wasn't time to wait.

Kahuna showed Friedman how to steer and control the sails. Mrs Smithies and Hunter helped load the food. Tusia and Sheldon took charge of the map.

As the boat pulled away from the shore, Ingham sat with Brodie in the stern. The water was crystal-clear in the moonlight. She leant forward and let her hand trail in the water. She was so hot and the water so cool against her skin. The silver of her bracelet flashed in the light of the stars.

'Tandi would have been very proud,' said Ingham.

Droplets glistened on her bracelet, smudging the

edges of the glyphs and leaking back into the ocean. A perfect silver circle, ending at its beginning, cupped her wrist.

'Mr Ingham,' said Brodie quietly. 'Did it worry you that the world thought you were mad for believing MS 408 could be read?'

The old man steepled his fingers in thought. She could barely see him in the moonlight. 'Being thought of as mad can never be a pleasant experience, Brodie.'

'But did it *matter*?' she said. 'Did it stop you doing what you knew to be right?'

'Never,' he said. 'Do you remember long ago, when we first tackled the codes of the Tower of the Winds? We talked about how breaking the coded language of MS 408 was like breaking the genetic code. Working out how men and women become what they are.'

Brodie remembered.

'And do you remember how we talked about that responsibility? How once we knew what had been said in MS 408, we had a duty to know how to act on it?'

Brodie did.

'Well, I guess we're acting now. We could have stayed at home and known what MS 408 was directing us to. We could have stopped there, but that was never enough, was it? Not for any of us. The pull of the code always wanted total completion for us. Always.' He looked around the boat. At the rest of the team. 'We're all here for a reason, Brodie. None of us could have left it as it was. We had to come here. However mad that would make us look in the eyes of others, we had to see for ourselves.'

'And what happens if, when we see,' asked Brodie quietly, 'we realise there's something else we must do?'

Ingham looked troubled. 'Then I guess we'll do what we have to,' he said.

They sat for a moment watching the wake of the boat. The lift of the surf as it pulled out into the ocean. A silver track, glistening in the darkness.

'Don't shut me out, Brodie.'

Ingham had gone below deck to take some seasickness pills and Friedman had taken the seat beside her. She was cold. She should be inside with the others, but she hadn't moved for hours.

'I don't know what you mean?'

In the semi-darkness she could see he arched his eyebrows. 'Don't play games. I can tell there's something you're not telling me. Why the sad face? We've done so well. We're nearly there.'

Brodie pulled the cuffs of her sleeves down over her wrists, fearing the bracelet would give her away. 'It's nothing.'

Friedman turned to look at the sea. 'You know there's something I want to tell you,' he said. 'Something about me and your mum and when we were young.'

The mention of her mother made her heart beat frantically in her chest.

'When we were children, no older than you, we lived at Station X.'

'I know,' said Brodie. 'You and Mum and Smithies. I've always known.' Was that all he had to offer?

'There wasn't just us though,' he said.

Brodie looked up.

'I mean, there were adults too, of course. But there was another child. A fourth child.'

Brodie couldn't believe what she was hearing. All the time, all the stories, there had just been the three of them. How could there have been a fourth? 'But the photograph,' she blurted. 'The three of you, in front of the huts at Bletchley. There was only three.'

'Three in the photo. One outside – with the camera.'

She'd never thought of that. 'Who was it? The other person?' she said.

'His name was Riley O'Shane. He was the same age as us. His parents were part of the Study Group. But we didn't like him.' Friedman lowered his head.

'We were only children. Cruel none the less. We left him out of our games, never told him our secrets. And all he wanted was to be part of our group.'

'What happened to him? This Riley O'Shane?'

'He became part of the government. Worked for the Ministry of Information. He did well for himself. He let nothing stand in his way.'

'Why are you telling me this?'

'Riley O'Shane became the Chairman of Information Services. He headed up the Suppressors. He runs the team that would have ended our search. The team that took your mother's life and Tandi's.'

Brodie balled her hands into fists. 'Why have you waited so long to tell me?' And then she remembered, that night in the Plough when they'd been working on the Dorabella Cipher, and she'd overheard Smithies and her granddad talking with Friedman. They'd spoken about leaving someone out and how her mother had suffered. This was what they meant. 'You're telling me that all this has happened – all the things the Suppressors have done – because of how you behaved when you were children?'

'Yes. No. I don't know. Riley wanted so much to be part of our team and we excluded him. Now he's having his revenge.'

Brodie's mind was churning like the sea.

Friedman looked scared, as if he'd lit a firework and hadn't time to run to safety. 'I'm just saying this search for Avalon is complicated. It's not a single story. There are other stories intertwined with ours and we've got to step back and make sure we see the bigger picture.'

Did he know? Had he heard what Kahuna had said about a price to be paid? Brodie plunged her arm over the edge of the boat and drew a handful of water up to her face. 'I'm tired,' she said.

He nodded awkwardly. 'Just know we're in this together, Brodie,' he said. 'All of us. D'you understand?'

She didn't. But her mind couldn't cope with knowing any more.

The storm was growing. Kerrith thought this was a good thing. It kept the Chairman below deck. Things were easier this way.

She gripped tightly to the handrail and walked backwards down the steps, pulling the hatch closed behind her.

The Chairman looked a little green, his eyes wide and watery. He was holding a drink. The liquid swilling like the ocean.

'I'm not sure that's the best idea, sir,' Kerrith said.

'I can't feel any worse,' he snarled.

Kerrith took the drink from him. 'But just to be sure.'

'Are *you* sure, Miss Vernan?' he said mockingly.

'Sir?' She didn't understand his question.

'Sure about everything, I mean. What we do. Why we're here.'

'You mean, here in the middle of the ocean, sir?'

'Yes. I mean in the middle of this ridiculous ocean, Miss Vernan.'

Kerrith steadied the glass but the amber liquid inside continued to lift and fall. 'I know why I'm here,' she said.

'Good. Good.' His pallor greyed a little. 'And Miss McCloud. You said she's sleeping. But she understands too, doesn't she?'

Kerrith looked down into the glass. 'She understands,' she said, and she kept her focus closely on the drink.

'Good. Good.' The Chairman wriggled in his seat but obviously failed to make himself more comfortable. 'Did you ever see the paperweight, Vernan?' he asked.

It was an odd question. 'Paperweight, sir?'

The Chairman wiped his eyes. 'The Director's. I thought it beautifully summed up our cause, don't you think?'

'The one with the sword in the stone, sir?'

'That's the one. Perfect image of all we're about. One overriding power able to withdraw the sword. It makes sense of all we do. It explains how we only do what is needed to be done.'

Kerrith was tempted to drink from the glass she held. 'We do what needs to be done,' she confirmed.

She couldn't help but remember though, when she'd looked closely at the Director's paperweight, that her hand as well as his had withdrawn the sword. The idea that only one was capable of the task had been a deception.


'What is that?'

They'd taken it in turns to sleep, although the boat was listing so far to the side that even tied into the bunk by a lee sheet, Brodie couldn't rest. She pulled herself out of the cabin and on to the steps that led to the deck. Hunter was with Friedman at the wheel.

'The sparks?' answered Hunter, looking up at the blue and purple flames that seemed to be shooting from the tip of the mast. 'Sicknote says they're called St Elmo's fire.'

'St Elmo?'

'Patron saint of sailors,' said Hunter.

The air crackled and buzzed. 'And we're doing

nothing about them?' asked Brodie, looking up at the bright-blue balls of light bouncing above the sails.

'Nothing we can do,' said Friedman. 'They're caused by volcanic eruptions under the sea. Pigafetta wrote about seeing them. And Shakespeare even wrote about them in *The Tempest*.'

Brodie remembered. 'And they're a good thing?'

'Depends who you ask,' said Friedman, leaning his weight on the wheel. 'Like fire in general. It can be good. It can be bad.'

'I don't like it,' said Brodie, moving up on to the deck.

'Me neither,' said Hunter.

Friedman turned the wheel a little to the left. 'They're scary. But they make me feel alive.'

Brodie looked out to sea. There was no sign of land in any direction. The wind was lifting. She felt cold. 'Will we be OK?'

Friedman took a while to answer. 'We should change the spinnaker. Make the most of the wind,' he said. 'If the storm's picking up, we need to get it to work on our side.'

Brodie didn't like hearing him use the word 'storm'. She didn't like him talking about sides.

'We should get the others up,' he added. 'Time we were all awake.'

It took a while to walk along to the sail store at the end of the boat. Hunter held her hand as she manoeuvred along the deck. The boat strained over. The splash of the sea was salty on her lips.

'Why didn't we get the job of waking the others, instead of the job of changing the sail?' Brodie moaned, as Hunter clutched tight to the handle of the hold. 'Anyone could have shouted "all hands on deck".'

'Take it easy, B.' Hunter laughed. 'You don't need to get so uptight.'

It was fair to say, Hunter's opinion had never, in all the times she'd known him, been more wrong than on this occasion.

The sail hold was like a long cupboard at the bow of the boat. The door opened like a hatch. It was possible to see the hold was packed with sails. It was also possible to see there was someone hiding there.

'What the fig biscuit?'

Fire crackled at the tip of the mast, lighting the sky with a violet glow. The boat lurched to the left and Brodie fell forward towards the hold. Face to face, eye to eye, nose to nose with another human.

She heard screaming. It took a while to realise that she was the one making the noise. Brodie scrabbled backwards and Hunter grabbed her arm to steady her.

'It's OK, it's OK,' he yelped, slamming the hatch. 'We're all OK.'

'We are so NOT OK,' yelled Brodie. 'There's someone in there. Someone real.' Even as she said the words she knew they sounded stupid, but she knew she was right.

Behind her, Smithies and Sicknote were scrabbling forward. 'Let me see,' said Smithies, forcing his way to the front.

Brodie clung on to Hunter's arm.

The hatch door swung open again and this time there could be absolutely no mistake.

There was someone there. That someone was Kitty.

'She's a murderer,' hissed Sheldon. 'A betrayer. We've got to get rid of her.'

'What are you saying?' said Friedman. 'We toss her overboard?'

'Yes. No. Of course not. But this is wrong. She can't be here.'

'But she is,' said Sicknote. 'Although how she managed to be here when we're in the middle of the Pacific is beyond me.'

The wind was ripping at the mast. The metal of the sail attachment clanging against the wood.

Kitty rubbed her face. 'I came to Kanton on the last

supply plane. I wanted to speak to you.'

'So you hid in a sail store! And were you just going to wait there? Until when?' Hunter was shouting now.

'Until it was the right time to talk to you.'

'The right time.' The words jarred in Brodie's throat. 'How can there *ever* be a right time for you to talk to us? After what you did?'

'It was all a mistake. I never meant to do any harm.'

'It doesn't matter what you meant,' Brodie spat. 'You led the Suppressors right to us and Tandi paid with her life.'

'I never meant that. And I'm here now to try and make up for it.'

'How can you possibly make up for what you did?'

Kitty stared hard, her face white in the sparking light of the fiery air. 'I don't know. I don't know. I just wanted to try. And for you to know why.'

'*Why?*'

'Why I did what I did.'

'And?'

Kitty lowered her head. She couldn't look at them. 'I just wanted to be part of something.'

A thought sparked in Brodie's mind. Friedman and the friend they'd left out. Riley. A man who went on to work for the Suppressors. Was it all their fault, then, that people betrayed them? Was it really down to them that people died? How could it be their fault when others had done something so wrong? The problem tore at her brain. 'You can't make this our fault,' she hissed. 'We *did* include you. Tandi more than anyone else wanted you to be part of the group and look at what you did to her!'

'But I never meant to and I'm trying to make it right. That's why I came. That's why I flew all this way and hid in this stinking hold. I came to try and make it right.'

'And how can you possibly do that?'

Kitty looked up now and this time she met Brodie's gaze. 'I came to warn you the Suppressors are on to you. They know where you are. They're tracking your boat.'

'We can't deal with her now,' said Smithies. 'If she's right and the Suppressors are on to us then that's what we've got to focus on.'

'But we've got to know whose side she's on,' yelped Brodie. 'It makes all the difference.'

'Is it that easy?' said Friedman. 'Really? Good and bad, right and wrong? Is it really how life works?' He ran his fingers through his hair. 'I was with your mother when she died, Brodie. And I failed her. I couldn't save her. Does that make me bad? For a while you thought it did. For a while you could only see what happened. You couldn't see why.'

'And knowing why doesn't make it all right,' she blurted. It was the first time she'd said so. The first time she'd tried to tell him, after all these months, that whether he was able to or not she still felt he should have saved her. That a part of her was still raw with the pain of knowing he'd failed. She gulped in air and clung to the handrail as the boat listed to the side.

'And I think that every day,' said Friedman. 'Every single day. I should have done more. But I can't be who I need to be now, or be any sort of father to you, unless I try to move on. We've all made mistakes, Brodie. Some of them huge. Some of them costly. But we've got to do all we can to try and make things right and move on. We've got to keep trying.'

'But how can we trust what she says? After everything she did?'

Friedman squeezed her hand. 'We just have to try.'

'You want us to forgive her?' she blurted, and her nose was running and the sea spray was whipping at her face.

'I think it's only when we forgive that we can actually move on,' he said quietly. 'Forgiveness and acceptance are sometimes the hardest things in the world.'

**Circle.172.4.9**

'But it's what Avalon's about,' whispered Tusia.

Brodie peered at her friend.

'Well, isn't it? Isn't that what you've been trying to tell us all along with all your stories and your legends? Avalon is for everyone, not the special few. That everyone counts.'

'But you have to mean you're sorry,' said Brodie.

Hunter turned his head. Kitty was sitting at the bow of the boat. Her head was lowered, her shoulders hunched. 'We have to believe she's sorry,' he said.

'But that takes trust. And we trusted her before.'

Hunter nodded. 'I know. But we've got to let her *show us* she's sorry.' And it was all he had time to say before the air was rent open with a mighty crack.

It was easy to see what had happened, and a rational part of her brain tried to tell Brodie to be calm. Panic wouldn't help.

The rational part failed.

The mainsail of the boat was attached to the mast by metal clips. These allowed the sail to fill with wind and pull the boat forward. The system didn't work well when the clips were tugged and wrenched in the wind. Sometimes they were ripped from the mast.

This wasn't necessarily a disaster. A sail fluttering slightly free from the mast would hinder the boat. It was a pain to re-attach. It slowed things down.

This was all true unless the wind was strong. And the boat was leaning. And the sail flapped in the water.

Unfortunately, all three of these things were happening now, and Brodie didn't need anyone to tell her this combination changed things. It made things very, very bad.

The boat was leaning heavily to the left and the sail, flapping free of the mast, played with the surface of the water first. It skirted the lid of the ocean, it scuffed up white waves. But then, in only seconds, part of the sail sank down below the water and began to fill.

It worked like a bag. The water flowed in and the bag grew heavier. And it pulled down further in the water. It strained against the mast. But the mast was rigid. It was unyielding. That was, after all, its job.

So the mast stayed tall and the sail sank down. And the water pressed heavy against the sail so the boat leant further and further towards the ocean.

The crack Brodie heard came from the mast. A slit ricocheted down the length of the pole. It struck the base like lightning, earthing down a rod. But the mast didn't snap. It was too strong. Instead, the sail sank deeper and the boat leant further and above them all the air glowed violet with St Elmo's fire.

Brodie scrabbled along the deck. She stretched over

into the water. She tugged at the sail, her fingers slipping and grappling in the water. The spray stung at her eyes and at her skin and the sail slid through her grasp like soap.

'Help me!' she screamed. 'Help me!'

Other hands worked with her. It was impossible to tell whose. The spray soaked her arms and her face and the boat stretched out for the water and the mast strained taut below the fire. But the sail sank deeper. Curled down towards the bottom of the ocean with a speed and an elegance which was almost beautiful.

'We've got to let it free,' screamed Tusia. 'We've got to let the sail free. It's going to drag us under. All of us. We've got to unclip it.'

But the sail was now too deep and the ocean too rough. And Brodie lurched and scrabbled at the fixings and the metal bit into her skin. Blood bloomed on the water like a red wreath above a white coffin, lowered deep into the sea.

'Cut it!' yelled Tusia. Her words ripped from her mouth and echoed on the wind. 'Cut it loose!'

But there was no knife. No blade sharp enough to slice the fabric. And still it pulled and the boat rolled further and the mouth of the ocean reached up at last about to take its prey.

Brodie wasn't sure who thought of the sword.

Pigafatta's gleaming gift from Avalon. The reason they were here at all.

She didn't know who brought it from the hold. She didn't know who passed it down the line of frantic hands working one with another. But she saw it now. Friedman held it and lunged against the fabric.

The sail buckled in the ocean. It opened its great white expanse to draw in more water. And the mast cracked and shuddered under the weight.

But Friedman drove on. He sliced at the fixings and he plunged the sword deep into the sail. And for a moment St Elmo's fire surged at the point of the blade. Her dad's face bright in the light of the fire.

And the mast strained and the sail lurched and then, in one fluid movement, the end of the mast severed and the sail was free.

And for a moment, all was safe.

The boat rocked back out of the water. Water spewed from the deck. The broken mast carved an arc of fire in the sky and the body of the boat juddered and shook as the sail and mast tip slipped free to a watery grave.

And it would have been over and they would have all been safe, if the boom had not swung back then like a giant arm through the air and crashed against Brodie's body. She buckled. The weight of the boom heavy on her side.

And the deck of the boat, safe under her feet, slid away.

She saw herself, reaching out. First Friedman, who reached out with the flaming sword. Then Hunter, his eyes wide. Then Kitty. And hands grabbed for her as she fell from the edge of the boat. And the sword flashed gold in the water. And a ring of fire circled her. And the discarded sail in the water reached up, free now of its weight of water and seeking something else to wrap around and pull down to the bottom of the ocean.

And it found her.

# 11

# Dark Side of the Moon

Brodie lay face down. Grit, or maybe sand, pressed into her cheek. She could taste salt in her mouth.

The sun beat down on her head. Water lapped at her feet and the sound of waves turning and turning without rest throbbed in her ear.

She opened her eyes.

Pulling herself up, the pain in her side overwhelmed her. The old wound from the caves of the Blue Ridge Mountains had been re-opened by the boom of the boat.

She understood then, she was on a beach. A long golden beach stretching further than she could see. Behind her, an enormous ocean. In front of her, bare land rising up towards a small lagoon. Birds played at the edge of the water there. They called out to the wind but they paid her no attention. She was, to them, a piece of driftwood washed up on the shore.

Brodie swivelled her body round so she could sit. A red stain marked the sand but her side was no longer bleeding. The skin around the wound was puckered and wrinkled like the tips of her fingers. She'd no idea how many hours she'd been in the ocean, but it had been a long time. It was like the beginning of her favourite play, *The Tempest*. Shakespeare's story that had helped lead them here. Now she was reliving it.

She shielded her eyes against the sun and saw the snapped mast and the sail. The shroud which had carried her, discarded now, like jetsam on the beach.

She looked out to the ocean. There was no sign of the boat. She was alone. Shipwrecked on an island in the middle of the sea. And there were only flightless birds to see her.

And then, out of the corner of her eye, she saw something tall. An awkward structure reaching up out of the sand. It looked out of place. Some sort of man-made tower.

Brodie stood up and began to walk.

As she drew nearer, the tower became clearer. A haphazard arrangement of stones piled one on top of the other. The stones looked grey from a distance, like faded slate, washed by the rain. But as she got closer,

Brodie could see the stones were not grey but coloured. Pinks and blues and greens, fluid colours, twisting and stretching in the light of the sun. She'd seen stones like these before. The stone in the necklace she wore around her neck. The stones on a ring. And the stones on the sword. Pigafetta's sword.

And then Brodie understood who'd built the tower on the beach. Pigafetta and Martin and Hans. The Knights of Neustria. A sign to mark this island as distinct from any other.

Brodie touched the stones and they were warm. Heated by the volcanic fires which forged them. Elfin Urim sparkling in the sun.

Brodie knew where she was.

She was on Arthur Island.

It was only then that Brodie heard the crying.

She peered into the distance, along the line of the shore, and she saw a seated figure hunched on the sand. Shoulders bowed, hair matted by the wind and the sea. Kitty.

Something like anger swelled inside Brodie. This was not supposed to happen. They were all supposed to find the island. Together. The team. Not the betrayer who'd done so much to let them down. Brodie didn't want to leave the tower of rocks. She'd didn't want to leave the promise of Avalon she'd longed for so many months and years to find, but the sound of the crying didn't lessen.

Brodie closed her eyes, hoping that by cutting out the sight, the sound would disappear too. But, if anything, the sound intensified, grew stronger in her ears.

She lowered her hand from the tower and began to walk across the beach. Her feet sank into the sand, marking her steps. And it was then she noticed the trail of steps stretched from the tower to where Kitty sat. As Brodie turned to check, she saw footprints led from where she'd first woken up on the sand. Brodie tried to make sense of the marks she saw and her mind could only make sense in one way. Kitty had been with her when they'd washed up on the shore. They'd come aground together.

By the time Brodie had made sense of the marks, she'd reached her. Kitty looked small, younger somehow, like a child and not a woman. Her shoulders were bowed as if she was waiting for punishment from above. She didn't lift her head as Brodie came close. She simply clutched her face, clearly wanting to stifle the crying but without knowing how. And Brodie saw her hands were bleeding, her nails broken and jagged.

Brodie knelt in the sand. Only then did Kitty look up.

And without any words and only the scars on her hands and the sound of her sobs, Brodie knew what had happened in the water. She understood Kitty had saved her. That as she'd fallen into the sail, Kitty had fought to free her from the fabric twisted around her. And somehow, when all was dark to Brodie, Kitty had clung to the broken mast and steered them to the shore.

'I never meant to hurt anybody,' Kitty said. 'You have to believe me.'

'But you joined with the enemy.'

'But I didn't understand.'

Brodie didn't know how to answer. 'Why did you come back? Why would you try and find us and hide so long, like you did?'

'Because I understand now how it worked and I knew what I'd done was wrong.'

'But why hide? Why not tell us what you knew as soon as you came to Kanton?'

'Because I wasn't sure you'd listen. I came to Kanton with them because they tracked you. I saw how close you were and I wanted to tell you. And I thought if I let the boat leave Kanton and hid inside, you'd have to listen to me. But then, in the hold, I was scared of what you'd do to me. I was scared saying sorry wouldn't be enough. And then I was worried I was too late.'

And then something weakened inside Brodie. She believed Kitty. It didn't make what Kitty had done right. It didn't excuse Tandi's death or make it easier to bear. But Brodie couldn't hate her any more.

'You saved me,' Brodie said at last.

'Because I knew you had to find Avalon before they did.'

'What do you think they'll do? The Suppressors, I mean, if they find Avalon?'

'They're capable of anything. I know that now.'

Brodie listened to the ocean moving backwards and forwards like a beating heart. 'I think it's here,' she said. 'I think Avalon's on this island.'

'Then you have to find it.'

'And you?'

'I'll keep watch,' she said. 'You should do this alone.'

Brodie untangled the broken mast tip from the discarded sail and walked towards the centre of the island using the mast for support.

It was clear to see the lagoon was heart-shaped, stretching across the centre of the island. Smooth

243

water shone like the surface of the mirror, rippling only when disturbed by the birds who waded round the edge. They raised their heads as she approached, as if they'd been expecting her. Not a single one opened their wings to fly. Their scarlet and turquoise feathers rippled like the waves.

Brodie looked down and the water mirrored back a face she barely knew.

She thought back to the time on the bridge in the village years ago, when her face had reflected back to her from the ruffled and disturbed waters of the river. Straw-coloured hair and crooked teeth, the face of a child who she was sure then wasn't big enough to make a difference to anything. Now she was on Arthur Island, on the edge of Avalon.

To her left, the lava had piled and folded like a steep bank, protecting the lagoon. But as the water washed backwards and forwards she could see, in the centre of the ring of lava, an opening like the mouth of a cave.

It was too far to swim. If she circled the lagoon she wasn't sure she would be able to climb down to the opening. She needed a way of crossing the water.

And then, to her side, the flock of birds moved slightly and she saw the edge of a small wooden boat, discarded there, or maybe waiting.

The boat was old. Brodie wasn't sure it was watertight. But it seemed the safest way to cross the lagoon. So she dragged it down from the sand, and then, using the mast as a paddle, she began to steer herself across the water.

Spray splashed against her arms and the sun beat down. Her arms ached but she kept on.

At last, the rising bank of lava cast a shadow across the water. The opening to the cave was clearer now and the end of the mast rammed against the bottom of the lagoon. Brodie steered to the side and directed the boat into the opening. Sand rushed up to meet them and the boat slid to a halt, carving a line in the sand.

Brodie rested the mast on the floor and levered herself out. Then she pulled the boat further into the cave and out of the water.

The ground was smooth, weathered and washed by the water over centuries. It felt like glass under her feet. Yet it wasn't cold as she expected but warm, heated from inside like the stones in the tower by the shore.

After several steps forward, the surface on which she walked changed levels, opening out into steps which led down.

And then the steps widened into a tunnel but it wasn't dark. Light seemed to emanate from the walls.

Crystals pressed into the lava formed the passageway in which she walked. The fire of the volcano she knew had formed the tunnel still burned inside the stones she saw.

Her footsteps echoed on the ground, matching the beat of her heart.

And then, quite suddenly, as the tunnel began to broaden and the colours on the wall grew even brighter, Brodie sensed, as she'd done on the beach, that she wasn't alone.

This thought didn't scare her. It wasn't the Suppressors. She knew that. It was someone else. Someone who belonged.

And then, from the widened end of the tunnel, a woman stepped forward. She was dressed in white, her hair long and flowing and her face soft, her eyes bright. She looked at Brodie as if she'd been waiting just a little while to welcome her. She reached out her hand and it too was wrapped in white. And Brodie remembered Tennyson's poem when this had all begun, and the hand in white samite he described as it passed King Arthur his sword.

Brodie knew who this was and she wasn't afraid. 'You're the Lady of the Lake, aren't you?' she said.

The woman smiled. 'Welcome to Avalon,' she said.

* * *

'How could I have been so stupid?' blurted the Chairman.

Kerrith stood her ground.

'She was willing to betray her friends. So why not us?'

'Sir. You should try to keep calm.'

Sea travel hadn't agreed with the Chairman and a vein was bulging rather dangerously at his temple.

'You see, once someone is willing to betray it's a hard habit to break.' He was snapping and the vein was throbbing. 'You saw no sign of Kitty's impending disloyalty?' he blurted.

Kerrith shook her head.

'But no matter.' The Chairman was drawing strength from his anger. 'This isn't over. And the brilliance of the plan is all down to location and timing.'

'Sir?'

The Chairman drew himself up tall. The boat rocked slightly, responding to his movement. 'We're in the middle of nowhere, Kerrith. Straddling the International Date Line. It really doesn't matter if Kitty has double-crossed us. Disasters here can be wiped away in the waters of time. Simply washed away.' He laughed at his own joke. 'History is brilliant like that. Whatever happens here can be "vanished" if we want it to be, and that's why it was so very short-sighted of that team of has-beens and wannabes to come here. After all their years of running and searching, they've finally made a fatal mistake. They've fallen through the loop. Like all those at Site Three.' He laughed again. 'Underground. Out of sight. Nothing of importance happens there. And here it's just the same.'

Kerrith considered all he said.

'You know history is very good, through the power of the Tyrannos Group, at clearing up her mistakes. I like the story of Valentin Bondarenko. You know it?'

Kerrith tried to shake her head.

'He was training to be a Russian cosmonaut in the 1960s. His photograph was taken with the other trainees. But he made a mistake. An error in training. It involved fire. And he died.' There was no compassion in the man's voice. No sense of loss. 'Tyrannos didn't want to have people scared. Revealing loss of life might have unnerved the public, so better all round to pretend that Valentin Bondarenko had never existed. His image was air-brushed from the photographs; his name struck from the records. He was "vanished".' The Chairman's lips stretched into something resembling a smile.

'Team Veritas should never have touched MS 408,'

he continued. 'They should never have discovered all they have about the Knights of Neustria. We've been trying for years to vanish their mark on history. What we do at the Black Chamber is important, Miss Vernan, and if there are casualties along the way, then so be it. We've come this far and if that crazy team of misfits think they've found something important then we will find it too. And we will control it.' He thrilled at the anger in his own voice. 'That's what all of this is about. Control. Do you understand?'

Kerrith nodded to show she did.

She understood far more than the Chairman realised.

She'd lied when she'd said she had no idea what Kitty was up to.

She'd heard of the Russian cosmonaut. She understood history had tried to wipe his story from the record. But she also realised it had failed.

There was a crater, she knew, on the dark side of the moon, named after Bondarenko. The man who had made a mistake and paid with his life in a terrible fire.

It seemed for those who'd made mistakes, there was sometimes a second chance.

# 12

# Circle of Fire

'So this is Avalon.'

Brodie stood at the end of the tunnel which opened out into a light and airy cavern. The space extended on, further than the eye could see, canopied by a sparkling sky.

Around the edge of the space, flowers grew. Flowers she knew, not from the world she'd left behind, but from the pages of MS 408. Heavy-headed sunflowers, plants with star-shaped leaves, multi-headed roots and tubers. Along the ground scuttled tiny creatures, bright with colour, and in the distance was a sight that made the air catch in her throat.

The castle.

A tall fortress with a central tower. Windows

reflecting back the light of an orange sun.

Brodie knew this place. She'd known it for years. This was the place of Voynich's manuscript.

The Lady of the Lake squeezed Brodie's hand. 'My name's Saraide. Come with me,' she said quietly.

And so they walked together, through fields of flowers and plants of the most dazzling colours Brodie had ever seen. Neither of them spoke. There was no need.

When they reached the castle, Saraide led the way inside. She took Brodie to a room in the tallest tower so they could sit and look out. Then she took a tall, thin cup of red and blue and gold like the ones Brodie had seen in the pages of MS 408. She lifted the lid. 'You should drink,' she said. 'I'm sure it's been a long journey. Why don't you tell me your story?'

When the story was told, Saraide refilled Brodie's cup. 'Let me tell you about Avalon now,' she said. 'This is the ninth isle, connected to the others by causeways of coral. What you see from here are the wonders Pigafetta recorded so accurately in his book of secrets. Of course, most people in your world believe his drawings show simply a place of the imagination. And in a way they're right.'

'But this place is real, isn't it?' said Brodie. 'What I

can see, is actually here?'

'One doesn't necessarily equal the other.'

Brodie didn't know what she meant.

'These isles are an enigma. You have an appreciation of that word?'

Brodie knew what an enigma was. It meant puzzle or riddle. Hadn't all their work to find Avalon been about riddles and puzzles?

'They straddle something your people call the International Date Line. Strange things happen to time and reality here. It's possible to reach the islands of the phoenix and leave them before you've even arrived. For the records of time to never show you've been. A natural time slip that exists without dispute and is accepted the world over. It's the first stage of the secrecy that protects this place.'

'The first stage?'

'Of course. There are two more circles of secrecy which keep us hidden here. The second is the protection the volcanoes and tide provide. Lava drifting and shifting so that the place is always unplottable. Determination is needed to find Avalon. But an element of chance too. The right tide. The right time. It all plays a role.'

Brodie thought back to the garden at Yale University. The structure of stone – one a cube balanced on its corner. She hadn't understood then how chance would play a part in her search. But it had, she realised now, always been important.

'And finally the circle of secrecy I know you understand well,' Saraide went on. 'The Knights of Neustria hiding our existence in codes and stories and signs. Time and geography and brotherhood. The power of three levels of secrecy keeping us safe from the world you've left behind. And does this all make what happens here unreal? That's up to you to decide. A writer from your world once said, '*It's not down in any map. True places never are.*' So you ask if Avalon is *real*. I can tell you only that it's *true*.'

Brodie looked out of the window, trying to take on all that she had heard. To the left of the castle she saw women walking beside lengths of what looked like tubes and pipes, connecting and twisting their way towards vast pools of emerald water.

'And is this place perfect?'

'People aren't perfect, Brodie. But this place is special. A magic exists here because *everybody matters*. That's the key. Everyone has a voice. We do all we can to treat people fairly here. History is full of attempts to build great things. Building together brings power, and so what we do here might to others seem scary or strange. It certainly scared the Creator when all types of men worked together to build a huge tower.'

'You mean Babel?'

Saraide looked impressed.

'Working together, anything was possible. And so the Creator separated men from one another in their understanding. He shattered the Earth in the ocean and spread the islands far and wide. People are so much easier to manage if they don't understand.'

'But Avalon survived?' said Brodie.

'Yes. And the stories about what this place is have changed with the languages of the nations they have reached. But its truth remained. Its veritas.'

The word made Brodie's heart race.

'Whatever name this place takes, whatever tales are told, its truth is that Avalon is where people live well. Together.'

'And Pigafetta and Martin and Hans came here long ago?' asked Brodie.

'They did. People had been hoping for the truth of this place and those three men came and saw for themselves. Just like you.' She hesitated for a moment. 'But you know that others have tried to find us. And their intentions have not been good.'

'We call them the Suppressors,' said Brodie.

'And they are the reason for those circles of secrecy. It is better people believe in the *truth* of this place than its *fact*. Do you understand that?'

Brodie wasn't sure she did.

'Avalon existing is like a pole star to people who would try and live well. People need to know the idea is possible. They need to strive for the truth of Avalon in their own lives. They don't need to see it to believe.'

'So were we wrong to come, then?' blurted Brodie.

'No. Not wrong at all. If the work of the Knights is to continue, we need those in every generation who strive to see for themselves and work to keep the truth alive. If seeing Avalon helps your team do that when they return, then all is well. And besides, the secret messages left by the Knights of Neustria which led you here were part of a stream of connections put in place in case Avalon was ever at risk and needed help, so it is good you came.'

'Needed help? In what way?'

Saraide took a deep breath. 'Avalon is always at risk of discovery. We know that. It's always at risk of damage too. Being here surrounded by a ring of fire means that at any moment the land could be shaken, the fires of the volcanoes that form diamonds and keep this special place hidden could suddenly overwhelm us.' She turned to look out of the window, considering whether to go on. 'I'd like you to spend longer here.

To meet with people and to talk and to see how things are done. But I'm afraid that time and geography are against us.'

'What does that mean?'

'The shifting lava reveals the opening to Avalon only occasionally, Brodie. There are times when the ring of fire closes the door you found and cuts us off from the world completely. I sense with the shifting of the tides, the recent storm and the fires in the sky that very soon the way across the lake will be barred for a while.'

'So I can't stay here long?'

Saraide's eyes darkened slightly. 'I think we have only hours before the opening to Avalon is sealed. Three hours at most.' She was looking from the window as if making calculations based on what she saw. 'So there's something else you should know about the risk to this place before our time together runs out. For there's another thing that could overwhelm us. A risk of something from within. Sorrow.'

Brodie knew all about the dangers of being overwhelmed by sadness.

'If this is a place where everyone matters, then hurt to one person, no matter who they are, hurts us all. Do you understand that?'

Brodie was trying to.

'There is something in our history here that has damaged us and which we've never recovered from. Years ago now, too many to number, an event that marked us. If I tell you the story, I'm afraid I may have to ask something of you in return. Are you sure you want me to go on?'

This was it then. Where Saraide would explain what Kahuna had warned her would be asked. 'I'm ready,' said Brodie.


'The story is about fairness and completion,' said Saraide.

Brodie remembered the circle Kahuna had drawn on the sand.

'I understand that completion's been the thing that's driven you. Spurred you and your friends on. To find this place when all others gave up, when even the most brilliant of brains failed.' She paused, dipped her finger a moment into the cup and then traced a circle of water on the tabletop. She looped the ends together and retraced the shape she'd made, covering every gap and join. A circle without an end. 'You tried to find answers to your puzzles and however complicated the clues and however tricky the riddles, you didn't give up. For all of you, it was about the end of the story, not just the beginning.' She waited a moment and they watched as the circle she'd drawn evaporated, leaving only droplets behind. 'So many walked away from Pigafetta's books and didn't see the story he was telling. So many walked away from the clues of the Knights of Neustria and didn't bother to find the ending to the tale. But you and your friends were different. You've followed the trail to the end of the story.'

'And how does this story end?' said Brodie.

Saraide's eyes were pools of ever-changing light. 'Its ending depends on the stories of others.'

'Whose stories?'

'Firstly, Arthur's.'

'King Arthur's?'

'It would make sense, don't you think? Complete things nicely if your story mirrored his?'

Brodie wasn't sure. 'But didn't Arthur die?'

'Eventually,' said Saraide. 'Although that's hardly the point.'

Brodie wasn't sure that could really be so.

'Arthur was returned to Avalon in his death. It meant his story could go on and on. It could live for ever, if you like, so his death wasn't really so important.'

Again Brodie wasn't sure she could agree. Death seemed pretty important in the scheme of things.

'But before he died, he called on his very closest

friend. You remember his name, don't you, Brodie? It's vital to your story.'

'Sir Bedivere.'

'Our very first Knight of Neustria. The very beginning of the puzzles and the riddles and the enigmas. The original phoenix. You remember what he had to do before Arthur died?'

'He had to return the sword to Avalon,' she said.

'A thought that scared him, you'll remember. Caused him to lie.'

Brodie remembered. Three times the King asked his knight if he'd returned the sword and only at the third time did he actually cast the sword into the lake.

'When the task was complete, Arthur could return here. The sword and an orphaned child who'd been brave and strong and tried to pass on some of the hopes of Avalon to your world, reunited here. We helped Arthur but he helped us too. A sense of working together is what keeps Avalon strong.'

Brodie thought she understood. Arthur needed Avalon but Saraide seemed to be saying that Avalon needed him.

'Centuries later,' said Saraide, her voice slightly hushed, 'the sword was given to another. You know now his part in the story.'

'Pigafetta?' said Brodie.

Saraide nodded. 'A visitor to our land whose name was written in the place of Arthur's on the sword. A new king, of sorts. But the world rejected Pigafetta and his stories and the sword was stolen eventually. But the sword wasn't the only thing to leave this place.' Her voice was grave now. 'Years after Pigafetta and his men came to Avalon, a boat travelled from Spain. The *Covadonga* docked at Arthur's island and only two travellers made their way to our shore. A sailor and a young woman who had smuggled herself aboard determined to find adventure. The sailor sought treasure but for the woman the greatest treasure wasn't gold and precious gems, although they took many of these things with them. No, her most precious treasure was life from Avalon. She took a child.'

Brodie knew they had got to the part about Renata. 'You're saying that Lucia stole the baby?'

'Yes. Being taken from this place cut short Renata's life. It was a terrible waste. An agonising loss to us. And the past shapes us. I'm sure you understand that.' She hesitated for a moment. 'Avalon *works* because of balance and fairness. Because everybody matters. The stealing of the sword and the child affected Avalon badly. It threw it off balance and I'm afraid that the balance has never fully been restored.'

'So does that make things no longer perfect here?' asked Brodie.

Saraide thought for a moment. 'It weakens its magic. It makes Avalon sad.'

Brodie wasn't quite sure how to phrase what she wanted to say. 'But it was so long ago. Renata being taken, I mean.'

'You think we should have moved on then?'

'Maybe?'

'Perhaps you're right, Brodie. But as I have explained, time works differently here. For us centuries ago seems like only minutes. And if your society is built on the idea that everyone matters, then you can see that an attack on that belief would still cause pain.' She traced a circle once more on the top of the table. 'There has to be some sense of making things right.'

'An apology, you mean?'

'That isn't always enough.'

Brodie didn't know what to say.

'Something must happen before the lava cuts us off from the world for a while. While the door is open, there's a chance for repair. If Avalon depends on completed stories, then I think perhaps you've worked out for yourself what will ensure Avalon's balance is restored.'

Brodie looked down at the ground. She thought of

the hours of puzzle solving and the stories they'd read and the clues they'd followed. And it was as if they'd all been simply training and preparation for this the final puzzle. Her mouth was dry. She could barely breathe.

'Have you worked out how this story must end?'

'You want the sword of Avalon returned,' she said quietly.

'Very good. And what else do you think is needed to complete the circle?'

And Brodie understood what she was asking. She knew at last what her promise to Kahuna would really mean. 'You need the return of a child.'

Brodie hurried down the tunnel. She counted her steps as she'd counted the tiles in the hidden corridor of the Royal Pavilion. She'd done it then because Hunter would have done so. It hadn't helped her then. She wasn't sure it helped her now.

The walls flickered and shone with the crystals which lined them. The air was heavy and still.

So much of what Saraide had told her confused her. There were three threats to Avalon. The fire that bubbled always under the sea. The Suppressors finding the island and destroying it. But there was also a threat from within. A sadness caused by a loss long ago that was left unresolved.

One thing was absolutely clear. That wasn't the ending to the story she wanted. All the puzzles and the clues and the riddles were about protecting Avalon, not destroying it. Everything had been about keeping Avalon safe.

So now, there was only one ending that was possible. The others had to find her. She needed Pigafetta's sword. She had less than two hours now to return it before Avalon was cut off from the world again. The rest of the promise she couldn't even think about. A stolen child. She closed her eyes for a second, trying to block out the thoughts that rammed against each other in her head. If what she believed was needed, would she be strong enough to do it?

The tunnel narrowed and for a moment Brodie thought she could hear sighing. But as she listened she realised it was the sound of the lagoon, moving in and out at the opening of the cave. The light brightened and the ground rose up in front of her.

The boat was waiting. She pushed it down the sand and then clambered inside, grabbing the broken mast and paddling forward.

Brodie turned. The waters lifted up behind her. She drove the mast down into the water and the boat left a rippled wake as she steered it onwards.

Once at the far shore she dragged the boat from the water.

The flightless birds barely noticed her. One bird only, with scarlet feathers, lifted his head. His eyes were the colour of sapphire. His stare piercing. Then, like the others, he looked away.

Brodie glanced down to the beach. It was darker than when she'd first stepped on the sand but it was clear to see what had happened. Kitty, who'd waited so long, wasn't alone.

She felt a surge of relief and excitement.

Then her happiness turned to confusion.

Two boats were anchored just off the shore. One scuffed and damaged by the sea, its mast broken, its sails torn. The other looked brand new, undamaged in any way.

A gaggle of people stood on the yellow sands. Sheldon and Tusia, Friedman beside them, and Smithies and his wife, Granddad and Sicknote and Kitty too. Brodie scanned the line. There was someone missing. The team incomplete.

Brodie masked her eyes against the glare of the sun and she scanned the shoreline. And then it was clear. To the side of the team, set back a little further from the sea, stood Hunter. His back was arched, his head raised up towards the sky. And at his neck something glinted in the light. Something gold.

Brodie staggered forward.

Hunter wasn't on his own. He was being held away from the others against his will. By a man. A man Brodie didn't recognise. A man who held a sword. Pigafetta's sword.

And the reason Hunter didn't walk away was very clear to see.

The man was holding the blade of the sword against Hunter's throat.

# 13

# Blinded by the Light
## of the Sword

'So your team's complete?' the man who held the sword called out into the wind. 'Alex's child! I suppose you're sick of people saying you look like her.' He swallowed a laugh. 'But you do.'

Brodie stumbled down the beach. Who was this man? Why was he holding the sword? 'Let Hunter go!' she screamed.

Friedman lurched forward and pulled Brodie into his arms. He held her so tight she could hardly breathe. She'd forgotten that, until they'd spoken to Kitty, they must have supposed she'd drowned. 'It's OK, Brodie. It's OK,' her father mumbled into her hair.

'How can it be OK?' she screamed. 'He's got Hunter.'

'And he's going to let him go,' hissed Friedman. 'If we're all very calm.'

Hunter gulped. The sword pressed against his throat. 'Best not upset him, B,' he mumbled. 'Not feeling perfectly happy about this.'

The man pushed Hunter's body and the point of the sword pricked into his skin.

Brodie pressed her fists against her mouth and choked back a scream. 'Who is he?' she garbled. 'What's he doing?'

Friedman took her hands down from her face. 'This is Riley,' he said. 'You've heard me talk of Riley. Seems he got word and didn't want to miss out on our little trip.'

So this man was a Suppressor. *The* Suppressor. Her mother's childhood friend who had wanted so much to belong. The man her father had warned them they'd excluded from the group. And he'd gone on to build a team of Suppressors intent on destroying stories.

And he'd followed them here, to the middle of nowhere, in the hope he'd find Avalon too. And if he found Avalon, things wouldn't end well.

Brodie shot a glance at Smithies. He raised his hand, pleading for her not to speak. Afraid she'd make the situation worse.

She could feel Friedman twitching beside her,

hunting for words Smithies was too scared to use. 'Riley was about to let Hunter go,' he said quietly.

Something beyond anger flashed across the stranger's face. 'You see, always the one to tell me what I think and what to do,' he hissed. 'You never change, do you, Robbie? Even after all these years and after all your loss, you still believe you can tell me what to do.'

Friedman stepped closer. Hunter flinched. 'Isn't that what you do now, Riley? Tell people what they can and can't think? Tell them what stories to believe and whose stories have a right to be heard?'

'Don't talk to me about rights to be heard!' the stranger yelled. 'What about my rights as a child? What about my right to be part of it all?'

'We were children, Riley. We knew no better.'

The man made a noise like a laugh. 'And yet you use children now. Children in your team when I wasn't good enough to be included. Look at you all. A ragbag collection of has-beens and wannabes.'

'But a team who worked, Riley. A team who found the truth after all these years.'

The man trembled. Then he tightened his grasp around Hunter's body, making him call out in pain. 'What truth?' the man cried. 'There's nothing here.' He spat his words. 'What did you hope to find in the middle of the ocean? Take a look around, Robbie. There's nothing but sand and water and birds that can't even fly.'

Brodie pulled free of her father's hold. It was possible then, just possible, that this man wielding the sword didn't know. He didn't see what she'd seen. He couldn't tell that beyond the lagoon, Avalon stretched out under them. There was a chance Avalon was safe. That he couldn't see the truth. That despite all the clues and the puzzles he still didn't believe what wasn't obvious to see.

None of this helped Hunter.

Riley pressed the blade firmly against Hunter's neck. A drop of blood bloomed from his skin. It rolled like a scarlet bead.

'Please let him go,' begged Brodie. 'Please.'

Riley raised his gaze to the heavens and when he looked down his eyes burned red. 'Why? Because he's your friend?'

'Yes. Because he's my best friend!'

'I have no time for friends. I learnt long ago they let you down. You're better off without them.'

He was wrong about Avalon and he was wrong about friends. Brodie knew they were the most important things of all.

But she swallowed the words she'd use to try and

make him understand. When telling her story could change everything, she did what the Suppressors wanted everyone to do. She used his most powerful weapon back against him. She said nothing.

She could hear Hunter's breath rasping in his chest.

Above, the night grew darker still and then the sky split open with a crack of light.

Seconds later thunder sounded.

The bead of blood splashed on to the sand.

Then the rain came.

The sky was the colour of spilt ink.

If Saraide was right, there was just over an hour left before the opening to Avalon resealed.

Brodie stumbled from her father's arms and her granddad reached out to hold her. 'Let him go,' she sobbed.

The sword pressed tighter against Hunter's neck.

Smithies broke free of the group. His eyes were hooded, his shoulders stooped, but when he spoke his words were soft, almost gentle. 'Please.'

'There's a word you must have heard a lot when we were small. *Please* let me join in. *Please* see I want to be involved.'

'The boy's done nothing wrong.'

'Neither had I, but that didn't stop your games and your taunts.'

'Can you really carry all that pain now?' groaned Smithies. 'After all this time?'

'I'll carry the pain until the day I die. It made me who I am.'

Smithies stepped a little closer. Riley pulled Hunter in more and Smithies raised his hands in surrender. 'And what you are? What you've become? Does it make you happy?'

'It has nothing to do with being happy. It has to do with being right.'

Smithies lowered his hands. 'Is this right? What you're doing now?'

'It's right I have my say. My people have followed you to museums and churches, graveyards and rivers. You and your ridiculous obsession with a book which should never be read. You've made my life difficult. Complicated everything. Do you have any idea how many lives have been involved in trying to stop your little game? I think it's time for payback.'

'But who decided you should be in control?' called Smithies, stronger now than Brodie had ever seen him. 'Who said you could take charge of what is read and what stories are told? Who gave you permission?'

'Permission?' Riley laughed the word. 'I don't need

your permission to ensure that only what is right is heard. And you have no right to interfere.'

'But the boy?' Smithies begged. 'Why harm the boy?'

'Because he reminds me of you!' The words hung on the air. 'Young and so sure of the answers. And life isn't like that. Answers have to be taught. By those who know.'

'And you know then?' snapped Smithies, his gentle voice hardening. 'You've made yourself the teacher?'

'Someone has to be in charge. Always.' His hand lowered a little and Hunter flexed his neck, but this movement angered Riley and he jabbed the tip of the sword tighter against Hunter's skin. A fresh bead of blood began to roll towards the sand.

There was another crack of thunder. The sky swirled with light. Brodie could hear Tusia sobbing but she couldn't turn away. Her attention was fixed on the blade of the sword. There was just under an hour left before the chance to return the sword would be lost. Both her best friend and the place they'd travelled so far to find were in terrible danger.

Suddenly another voice. Mrs Smithies this time, her voice as powerful as Brodie had ever heard it. 'You have to let go,' she said. Her words seemed to vibrate on the air. 'You can't hold on to this for ever.'

The sword shook a little.

'There will be people looking for us. People will know we've gone. They will come for us.'

'Not in this storm,' snapped Riley. 'This ocean is a maze of islands and lost lands. No one will notice your leaving. You won't matter. None of you, to anyone.'

'You're wrong,' said Mrs Smithies. 'We all matter.'

Riley laughed. 'To each other maybe. But to the world outside? Your stupid game is just a game. It makes no difference. *You* make no difference.'

'We make all the difference in the world,' Brodie said, anger lifting in her own stomach now. 'Please.'

'Please isn't the word I want to hear,' roared Riley.

The air rumbled. A third drop of blood fell to the sand.

'I know the word you want to hear,' said Friedman. 'The word you need is "sorry".'

The blade of the sword caught in the light of the storm. It lowered for just a second. The man turned his head. He looked out at the sea. At waves stretching and climbing and white horses racing in to the shore.

'We're sorry,' said Friedman. 'So very sorry. We were children and we knew no better.' Regret wreathed his face. 'But I understand it now. I see the power children have and I understand. We were wrong.'

Riley's sword hand swung down to his side. He still grasped Hunter tightly but the tip of the sword swung free of his neck and sliced towards the sand at his feet.

'We made a mistake,' said Friedman. 'And so many people have paid for the mistakes we made. But you chose your path, Riley. No one made you walk the road you took.'

What was Friedman doing? Riley had lowered the sword. Hunter was nearly free. Why would he anger the man now?

Riley angled his head to the side. The sword swung silently at his side.

'We're sorry for what we did. We were wrong. But nothing can excuse what you have done. Nothing.'

Brodie's heart quickened. What was he doing? She reached out, but her father pushed her arm away.

'Do you know what we call ourselves?' said Friedman slowly. 'This team of has-beens and wannabes you have spent so long trying to destroy?'

Riley didn't answer.

'Veritas.' Her father began to pace. His footsteps sinking into the sand. 'It means truth, and truth is what we've fought for. And you would know so little about that.'

'Friedman?' Smithies was reaching forward too.

'No, Jon. It's time he listened. Time our friend and the Suppressors he works for understood the value of the truth. For in the end it's all about the search for that.'

He looked down at Kitty and she hunched in shame at his feet. 'Truth hurts. Kitty betrayed us but she had no idea what she was doing. But with Riley,' his jaw was rigid, 'with him it was planned. We upset him as children. We ruined his time at Bletchley. And there's a truth in that. But what he did with that truth is inexcusable.' He drew in a breath to steady his words. 'We hurt him but the truth is, we didn't mean to. He's destroyed life after life. And that was his intention. Not a mistake. Not a childish game. It was deliberate and purposeful and planned.'

Brodie could barely breathe.

'He talks of rights and yet the truth is, he has no rights at all to do what he's done. Stories belong to the people who tell them. History is made up of stories from every race and every nation. He makes himself a god by confusing the stories and cancelling out those he doesn't like. And the truth is, that makes him worse than a child. It makes him less of a man.'

Brodie closed her eyes. Riley must be angry now. Surely, he'd re-raise the sword and slice it into Hunter's neck. It had to end now.

In the darkness of closed eyes, the sky lightened brilliant white. Thunder roared and rain, falling gently up till now, began to pour. It pummelled on to her skin and tore at the sand around her feet. She remembered how, long ago, she'd felt like she were standing on sand as it washed from under her. Now she really was. And with the beating of the rain, Riley's anger could only grow. She hid her face and held her breath. She couldn't bear to watch.

'The truth is,' yelled Friedman, and his voice was loud above the rain, 'there are no excuses for what you've done. No excuses at all.'

Brodie peered through her fingers as suddenly her granddad walked towards the sea. 'You have to make this right! Let the boy go and give me the sword.'

But the Chairman had no intention of doing either.


Riley raised the sword. The point shone in the light of a thousand stars. There was an explosion of violet light.

St Elmo's fire.

Blazing like a comet, the sword twisted and fell. Riley recoiled, clutching his arm to his chest and calling out like a wounded animal.

But the fire from the fallen sword didn't die.

Twisting and pulsing, the fiery ball moved closer to

the sea, as if drawn by magnets. And as it moved, the ground seemed to pull at Brodie's feet, sand collapsing under her, running free like grains through a timer.

The wounded man still clutched at his arm. Low guttural noises spluttered from his mouth, choking in his throat.

The ball of violet light pulsed above the water, beating like a heart, then it quivered for just a second. And exploded.

Shards of fire rained down like spears pummelling the shifting sand and lifting waves.

Riley drew himself up from the ground. His shoulders hunched, his hand blistered and bleeding, he ran towards the sea. Perhaps he hoped to reach the boat. Perhaps he made it there as the island trembled under the weight of the explosion. Brodie didn't watch to see. She was looking at the ocean. And she was scared.

There was half an hour left.

The water was on fire.


Brodie ran towards her granddad.

She grabbed his hand and held on tight. Fire burned in the sky around them, sparking so her granddad's face shone. He was framed in light, tall and protective beside her. Then the earth splintered. Sections rose up like icebergs in a winter sea and the sky, just for a second, darkened.

Brodie and her grandfather crumpled together, on to the sand.

Grit bubbled on Brodie's lips; rain pelted on her back and the heat of the fire singed at her hair.

Her granddad was beside her. His hand locked in hers. It was still. His fingers slack, loose in her hold.

'Granddad, please.'

But he didn't hear her. His eyes were unblinking, looking up towards a broken sky.

Brodie pulled herself to her knees. She grabbed his shoulders, lifted his arms.

His eyes didn't see her.

'No!' Brodie cried out. 'Granddad, no!'

And then Friedman was beside her.

He tried to pull her to him, cradle her in his arms, but she fought and pushed till she was free. And then she threw herself on to the unmoving body beside her and the sobs tore at her throat.

Behind her, the fire strained into the sky.

But her granddad's heart was still.

'Brodie, you should come away.' Friedman's voice was just a whisper.

Brodie couldn't breathe.

This couldn't be happening. She couldn't lose him. Not here. Not now.

'Brodie.'

How could Friedman understand? How could any of them understand?

She pressed her head down against her granddad's chest and she dug into the sand as the fire raged. But she was no longer afraid. She was angry.

And so, touching her granddad's face one last time, she drew herself up to stand. She walked across the shifting sands through the chaos and the confusion and bent down and picked up the sword.

It burned her skin. She didn't flinch. She felt no pain. She felt nothing.

It would have been easy now to leave what she'd promised to do. But now, perhaps, it was more important than ever.

Riley had been given a choice to make things right. He'd refused and now her granddad was dead.

She'd been given a choice too. And now she knew the decision which needed to be made.

There were only minutes left as Brodie walked to the edge of the lagoon.

# Nimrod and the Tears of Pele

Brodie knew the team called to her. Knew they were begging her to come back. But this wasn't about the team. This was about her and a promise and a sword.

This was something she had to do alone. And she had to do it now.

They'd never understand. They'd talk her out of it. But she was more sure than ever that this was what she needed to do.

The lagoon sparked with new flames.

And a new voice shouted in her mind. The voice of a story. And of all the voices she heard, this was the one she chose to listen to. '*Trust your heart if the seas catch fire, live by love though the stars walk backward.*' The words from a poem her granddad used to read her. She'd never really understood the words before. But then that was true of so much she'd tried to read in the last two years. Understanding, she knew now, came when it was needed. Even in death, then, her granddad wasn't silent. Through stories she could still hear him calling.

The water burned. The stars blazed. Her heart said walk on.

She remembered the diving board she'd walked along as a child. Long and narrow, stretching out into the unknown. Then, her granddad had called her and cheered for her. Now he called no more, only in her head. The walk she took this time she took alone.

When she reached the edge of the water the heat was overwhelming.

She searched for the boat but she couldn't find it.

She looked across the lagoon at the entrance to the cave. The lava bank was burning red, bubbling and steaming. She didn't know if she could reach it on her own. Wasn't sure if she'd get there before the entrance sealed itself. She had no choice but to try.

She tucked the sword into her belt and walked into the lagoon. Then she began to swim.

The point of the sword pressed against her leg but the water seemed to carry her onwards as if a tide was pulling her in. As if Avalon was helping her.

She could see the boat was wedged in the opening of the cave, and through the tunnel beyond she could see the tide had drawn back, revealing the land ringed by banks of fiery lava.

Visible now from the opening of the cave which acted like an archway, Brodie could see the brightest light she'd ever seen.

Brodie knew those on the beach could see it. Knew the drawing back of the tide curtain revealed the castle and the flowers and the world of Avalon which had been built on the coral reef.

And Brodie saw too that someone stood at the opening to the tunnel. A woman waiting for her.

Brodie tightened her grip on the pommel of the sword.

It was not the Lady of the Lake.

The woman was Kerrith. Enemy and Suppressor.

'And so, in the end, I must take the prize from a child.'

Brodie had heard those words before. In the Royal Pavilion when there'd been just the two of them. Then, Brodie had held the Firebird Box. The scabbard. The holder of the code. Now, she held the sword.

'How did you . . . ? Where did you . . . ?'

'On the boat,' said Kerrith. 'With the Chairman.

All the while you talked I was here. On the edge of Avalon.'

Brodie felt as if she'd been thumped hard in the stomach.

'I've seen now what you've seen,' said Kerrith, 'and I know how Avalon works and I know about the sword.'

Brodie hand's was heavy. The weight of the world hanging there.

'I know the entrance to Avalon will seal in less than ten minutes. I know the sword must be returned. And I know about the stolen child.'

Brodie lifted her arm. Tandi's silver bracelet burned on her wrist. A reminder of the circle. Beginning and no end. The need for return.

'You have to let me do this,' blurted Brodie.

Kerrith simply shook her head.

'But you don't understand.'

'I understand everything.'

'But unless the sword is returned, unless a child is given back then everything here will end.'

'I know.'

'So you have to let me do this,' begged Brodie.

Kerrith stepped forward. Her face looked younger than Brodie had ever seen it. Her hair was loose about her shoulders, her eyes alive with reflected fire. 'Before we end this, Brodie,' she said almost softly, 'tell me the story of the Lady of Shalott.'

'What? Are you mad?'

'Perhaps,' said Kerrith. 'Tell me the story of the Lady in the tower.'

This couldn't be happening. Her granddad dead and Avalon at risk and a woman who'd tracked them halfway round the planet demanding a story. 'No. I can't,' she sobbed.

Kerrith put her hand on the sword. The nails broken, uncoloured. 'I'll ask you again just one more time. Tell me the story of the Lady of Shalott.'

Brodie racked her brain for the sense of the story. She threw the words into the air in a tumbled mass. 'There was a lady locked away in a tower. And she could only see the world through a mirror.'

'Go on,' Kerrith urged.

'And one day she heard a voice. Lancelot's voice.'

'And where had Lancelot come from?'

'What?'

'It's important,' urged Kerrith. 'Where had he come from?'

'Avalon,' blurted Brodie. 'He'd been raised in Avalon. And the lady in the tower heard his voice and she wanted more than anything to see him. And she turned away from the mirror and she looked out at the world. And there was a boat. And she climbed in the boat. And she knew what would happen. Knew how it would end but she was drawn by the voice and she knew that after all the years in the tower, being out in the world for the shortest of times was worth it.'

'And?' pressed Kerrith.

'She gave up her life.'

'So the lady in the tower made a sacrifice for Avalon. And that's what you want to do.'

Brodie could hardly breathe. How could she give up all she knew and all she had and the friends she'd made? But the bracelet on her wrist rocked against her hand, the words of Pigafetta blazing in the light. 'Yes,' she blurted.

Kerrith lunged out for the sword. She tugged at the pommel and it slipped from Brodie's grasp. 'I can't let you do it.'

Brodie clutched at the air. Her prize ripped from her. 'Please! I'm running out of time!'

Kerrith stood tall, gripping tightly to Pigafetta's sword. Her voice was calm and metered. 'The sword's mine.'

Brodie was overwhelmed by a sickening fear. It was really over. Despite the years of challenging and

285

running and solving, the Suppressors had won. Kerrith had the sword.

But the fear swelled in her belly and she dug deep inside of herself to a place she wasn't sure was real. But it was true.

Memories flashed before her. Her mother reading to her; her granddad taking her to school; a boy on a unicycle knocking her to the floor; a triumphal archway and a pyramid tomb; a father lost and found; a circle of friends connected by a common cause. Brodie knew men who drowned saw their life flash before them. She saw hers now. And the heat from the fire beyond the opening to the cave was so intense she felt she'd drown in the flames.

But if this was the end, she wouldn't go down without fighting.

So she launched herself at the woman who'd done so much to destroy all they'd worked for. She scrabbled in the air as her body fell down the steps to the tunnel. She clutched at the sword, clung on to Kerrith's arm. And together they fell into the opening void.

The tunnel walls were warm. Brodie's back scraped along the wall, her arm splayed to the left. She heard the clink of metal. The scrape of sword on stone.

'Give me the sword,' Brodie begged.

Kerrith lifted herself from where she'd fallen. 'No!'

'But it has to be returned.'

The woman's face was soft not angry. A ring flashed in the light on her hand. 'I know. Saraide explained it to me too.'

'But you . . .' Brodie's words dried. This was making no sense. None of this. Why was the woman still here? If she wanted the sword, why hadn't she run back out of the tunnel and back towards the sea?

Kerrith winced and drew the sword into her lap. A trickle of blood ran down the side of her face and splashed on to the ground. 'It was never my intention to bring the Chairman here. You must understand that. With him we could make it this far. But it was Kitty's job to warn you. I was to keep him away. It was the storm that washed the boat off course. The volcanoes that brought the fire. But you know there were three dangers to Avalon and at least I can help you with the final one.'

'I don't understand,' said Brodie.

Kerrith cradled the blade like a child. 'Brodie, you were never like the woman in the tower. You never saw the world through a mirror. You lived life in the world. Always. You coped with the loss of your mum and being alone and with the puzzles and the codes. You connected with the world on every level. Through every story and every song and every picture and every

287

clue. But me – I looked only in the mirror. I was scared of life and the stories I heard and I left my friends and I left the world to be part of something which was only ever about doing a terrible wrong.'

Brodie sank to her knees. Outside she could still hear the roar of the ocean. The crash of the waves. The heat of the lava was building. Time was nearly up.

'You know, while you've been searching for answers, I've been searching too.'

Brodie had no idea what she was talking about.

'I found someone Level Five had locked away. A wonderful and compassionate and brilliant person. Someone who'd been my friend. Hantaywee went on to marry your friend Fabyan.'

Brodie remembered the woman in the airport. How did she connect to Kerrith's story?

But Kerrith was still explaining. 'I realise now I'm guilty of helping steal something away from Hantaywee which should never have been taken. She was locked away for trying to find the truth. Like Friedman and your mother and Tandi. All punished because they wanted to unlock secrets that had been hidden by those in charge.' She hesitated for a moment. 'So it should be me who pays this debt, not you. For the sake of my friend. For the sake of *your* friends.'

Brodie fought back tears. She couldn't think about her friends. She had to be strong.

'In trying to destroy all your team was doing, Brodie, I finally heard the story of Avalon. I can't begin to tell you how sorry I am about all I did.'

Sorry. This woman was sorry? But she'd taken the sword. It made no sense.

'I need to return the sword.' Brodie was pleading through tears falling without check.

Kerrith shook her head. '*Someone* needs to return the sword.'

'But a child has to do it. It has to be me.'

'But isn't seeing the world through eyes like a child possible for everyone? If they really try? Wasn't that one of the things Team Veritas learnt?'

'How do you know what we learnt?'

'From Kitty.'

'So what are you saying?'

Kerrith swallowed hard. 'I knew that truth. Long ago when I was a different person, I understood what it meant to have friends and how looking at the world with the excitement and wonder of a child was important.' She held out her hand. A ring sparkled on her finger. A small silver disc etched with the letter 'Z'. 'Hantaywee and I were members of the Z Society. We knew how things should be.'

'So what does that mean *now*?' Brodie pleaded. 'About the sword?'

'That it could be me who returns it. That it *should* be me.'

No. This was ridiculous. How could this make sense?

'You have to let me show you I'm sorry,' Kerrith said. Brodie's mind raced. Wasn't that what Hunter had said about Kitty? She needed a chance to prove change was possible. 'Don't I have a right to try?' Kerrith ploughed on, her hand raised to quash Brodie's interruption. 'I can do this. I *need* to do this. Your value is in the world, catching the stories and making sure they live on. You can't leave the team. They need you.'

Air caught in Brodie's chest.

'My chance to make amends is if I stay here, return the sword and make sure the balance of Avalon is returned. I'm not your enemy, Brodie. Not any more.'

Brodie tried to breathe slowly. The pain in her back seared and her arm was grazed and bruised. And as she looked down she saw the silver bracelet had snapped. It hung on her wrist. An open circle. She fumbled with her good hand. And the bracelet fell. And as it did, it closed. The circle reformed. It rolled to Kerrith's feet.

'Let me do this,' Kerrith said. 'This is the right way for the story to end.'

There was a surge of pulsating light. It seemed to sweep down the tunnel from the fiery lagoon and catch on the crystal of the walls and the folds of the lava on which Brodie sprawled. And for a second it was impossible to tell whether Avalon lay at the end of the tunnel in the distance or behind them in the blaze of light.

Brodie scrunched down against the wall of the cavern.

She squinted and saw Kerrith was standing, holding the sword, and the sword was glowing in the light with all the colours of the stones. And then, in the brilliance of the shine, Brodie saw a white-clothed arm reaching out. A hand which reached first the sword and then took Kerrith's hand in hers. Then in a swirl of mist, a curtain of lava fell like rain. Brodie could see no more. The door to Avalon had closed.

When she opened her eyes again, it was dark. The cavern was cold and all traces of the brilliant light had gone. Brodie could see the tunnel stretching into the distance but she couldn't see Avalon. The end was blocked like a cave. Lava newly folded, steaming gently, obscuring the view beyond. From behind she could hear the wash of the sea. A wave of overwhelming loss engulfed her.

She curled on her side, her arm pulled tight against her. And she leant her head back on the walls of the tunnel so her hair, still wet from the lagoon, hung loose behind her. She peered up at the roof of the tunnel, unsure what she hoped to see.

What she saw was light. Tiny beams of sun lasering through the rock. And the pinpricks of light speared down to the ground of the cave where they widened and spread, making a circle at her feet. A circle made by light through holes.

Despite her pain, Brodie smiled.

This whole adventure had started with light streaming through holes. Then, in a card to spell out an answer. Now, through rock doing the same. The circle was complete. Brodie lowered her head and let the light warm her.

Suddenly, she realised she was no longer alone.

Hunter stood behind her. This time, he was ringed by a light so bright she could barely see his face. But she knew it was him because she knew that of all of them, he would leave the others to look for her. And from her position on the ground looking up at him, the light haloed him as it had done that first day at Station X.

'Have I died?' she said.

Hunter crouched down beside her. 'Not quite,' he whispered.

'The sword,' she blurted.

He moved a lock of hair gently back from her face. 'Things had to be returned.'

He knelt beside her and pressed his finger gently to her lips to stop her talking. Then he scooped her into his arms and stood.

And he carried her, up the lava steps and to the entrance of the tunnel. The tiny boat was wedged on the sand. He rested her gently inside and then guided the boat into the water. For a second the boat flowed free without him. 'Come with me,' she said.

He waded into the water and jumped aboard. 'Always, Brodie.'

As they sailed across the lagoon he held on to her hand. Then when the boat had grounded on the shore of the lagoon he lifted her again into his arms.

And she leant her head against his chest as he walked because she knew she was safe now. And in her mind the sound of the sea and the people calling on the beach was like music. Like 'Nimrod'. And then for the first time she remembered what she'd forgotten she'd ever known. 'Nimrod' meant 'Hunter'. Perhaps the Knights of Neustria had known one day her friend would grow into the name which until now had never quite fitted him. They'd known he would be the one to bring her home.

If it wasn't for the loss of her granddad she'd have felt something like happiness as he carried her down towards the beach.

As the lagoon and the newly sealed entrance to Avalon slipped away behind them, a single bird with scarlet feathers crossed their path. It raised its head and looked at them. It was in no way surprised to see them. And then it opened its wings and flew.

The bird soared red against a cornflower-blue sky and it carved a circle in the cloud.

Hunter rested Brodie down on the sand and suddenly the others were around her, their voices excited and scared all at once. Mrs Smithies tended to her grazed arm and Friedman sponged her skin so the burning cooled. All the time, Hunter sat beside her.

When, for a moment, there was quiet, she asked him, 'Granddad?'

Hunter squeezed her hand. 'His heart, we think,' he said. 'With all the drama and the fire.'

Brodie saw the cut in his neck and the bloodstain on his collar.

'We carried him to the boat.'

Brodie couldn't find any words.

'We'll have him checked over when we get back to Kanton. If he takes things easy and gets the medication he needs then—'

'Medication? Kanton? What d'you mean?'

And there was a dawning then in Hunter's face. A wave of understanding. 'The storm and the explosion and the electrical charges are what did it, we think,' he mumbled. 'Sicknote was going on about something called Pele's tears. Some volcanic glass that fell. A sort of "resurrection effect".' He was hurrying his words but nothing he said made sense. 'The electrical charge in the glass that fell did something to his heart, like some sort of defibrillator. We don't know how. But it's OK.'

'But . . .'

'Your granddad's heart restarted,' he blurted. 'He didn't die, Brodie. He's alive.'

And so all she'd thought had happened hadn't been real at all. Kerrith hadn't stolen the sword for herself. Her granddad hadn't died. And they hadn't destroyed Avalon.

And the pain and the loss washed away as in the sky above her head a flightless bird circled like a phoenix risen from the flames.

# 15

# Return to Station X

They joined as one group to help Brodie down the beach and towards the battered boat.

Every part of her body ached and she could barely place one foot in front of the other. But as she relaxed into their help, a memory crept like a shadow over her.

'The Chairman,' she blurted. 'Where's the Chairman?'

Tusia was nearest. 'He's gone, Brodie.'

'How? Why?'

So Tusia explained. 'He was like some demented thing. The fire scared him. And the rising of the water. He couldn't cope with what he saw and so he ran. Out into the waves. We're sure he can't have survived. The ocean was so angry.'

'But did he see Avalon?' Brodie pleaded.

'No.' Tusia's voice suggested she was quite sure. 'He turned his back. All he saw was the sword and he was blinded by that.'

Brodie leant more heavily on those supporting her.

'The Chairman came all this way,' added Sheldon, 'but he never really believed. So he didn't see what we'd come so far to discover.'

'But you all saw?' urged Brodie.

'We saw,' said Smithies quietly. 'All of us.'

'And you know about Kerrith?' said Brodie.

'Kitty told us Kerrith had come to help and not to stop us,' explained Friedman.

Brodie steadied herself for a moment. 'She made the sacrifice. Someone needed to stay to make things balanced again . . . and she did that.'

'But why?' said Tusia. 'After all this time of being our enemy, what happened to make her do what she did?'

Kitty spoke slowly and Brodie had the sense the words were difficult for her to say. 'It was simple really,' she offered. 'She remembered her friend. It made all the difference.'

'That was all?' said Tusia.

'That was everything.'

Brodie looked round at all the friends who stood with her now. Her arm ached. Her side throbbed. She was exhausted but none of that mattered. It was as if standing with her friends she was like a sword protected by a scabbard. Like in the story of Arthur. It was the scabbard which was the most important thing. Always. The scabbard made you immortal. And Brodie wondered then if love from friends and family could do that. Make you stronger than death. Make you live for ever.

As the waves curled against the shore she was suddenly overwhelmed by a surge of love for the person now missing from the group who'd journeyed all this way together. The grandfather who – even when she believed he was dead – kept speaking to her through the stories they'd shared.

Brodie clutched tight to Hunter's arm.

Her best friend knew what she wanted.

He helped her carefully on board the boat to find her granddad.

Later Mrs Smithies strapped Brodie's injured arm. Brodie thought it odd how her injured arm felt weirdly disconnected from her and yet she'd never felt so connected to her friends on the boat. Like the Knights of King Arthur's Round Table, everyone had played their part. Everyone had helped in the quest. They'd been a team. And the truth she and Hunter had talked about back when they'd been on Fiji seemed more important now than ever. They would always be a team after what they'd been through together.

As evening fell and the sky burned red, Brodie stood by the rail of the boat. Water stretched further than the eye could see.

After a while, Friedman came to stand beside her. 'I'm so proud of you, Brodie,' he said.

'You are?'

He touched the locket still hanging round her neck. 'The castle,' he said. 'The thing your mother spent so long looking for. You found it. You fitted all the answers and the puzzles together, and you reached that place.'

The stone of the locket glinted in the fading light. Fire and water combined.

'Your mother would have been so proud too.' He turned to face the ocean. 'You know, you've done now what Hans of Aachen did. You've become so much more than how you started out. Hans was an orphan of the flames but he went on to be so much more.'

Brodie remembered how much she feared that was all she'd ever be.

'Hans was a finder of Avalon,' said Friedman, breaking into her memory. 'And now you are too.'

Brodie steadied herself with her one good hand on

the rail. 'I'm not really like Hans,' she said at last.

Friedman looked confused.

'Hans was an orphan,' she said quietly. 'I'm not. I have you, Dad.'

They stood in silence looking out to sea. The water lapped at the keel of the boat as it sliced the ocean and drove on. And in the darkening sky, stars shone brightly.

Eventually, Friedman broke the silence. He looked over to the seating at the back of the boat. Hunter was there. 'He's been waiting a while to talk to you.'

Brodie let go of the rail and her father helped her walk to the end of the boat. She sat down then Friedman left.

'You saved my life,' Brodie said at last. 'Again.'

'Yeah, well, you will keep getting yourself into these life or death situations and ploughing on regardless and someone has to come and sort you—'

'Thank you,' she interrupted him. 'For saving me.'

The hint of a smile pulled at the corners of his mouth. 'Anytime, Brodie. Anytime.'

For a moment they sat without talking. Then she fumbled with her good hand inside her pocket and drew out her second watch. 'It's a little scratched,' she said, 'what with the falling into the tunnel of a volcano. And I can't wear it now, what with the whole swollen arm situation. But anyway. I want you to have it.' She held it out and the glass face of the watch shimmered in the light of the stars.

'Your extra watch,' he said.

'I don't need it now,' she said. 'Time's moved on.' The words were hurting her throat but she knew it was important to say them. 'I've let my mum go and I'm ready to move on. Because I understand now, she's with me. I don't need to stop time to pretend she hasn't gone. She's inside me, like the castle inside the locket, and she's with me in every story I hear and every tale I tell.'

Hunter didn't move.

'Please,' said Brodie. 'I want you to have it.'

So he took the watch from her and he fastened it to his wrist. 'Thank you,' he said.

Again they sat in silence and watched the waves of the sea.

Then he turned and took something from his own pocket. 'I have something for you,' he said, and he held out the Jumbo Rush Elephant from Bletchley Park Mansion. 'I know you lost Tandi's bracelet. And so everyone thought you should have this. It's a reminder of how important the battle for good is. A reminder that lives are lost when stories are lost. It's kind of what you said about your mum, I suppose.

That we keep people alive in the stories we tell.' Even in the half-light, Brodie could tell he was blushing. 'I'm not as good at this as you. The whole story thing.'

Brodie took the elephant. 'You're perfect.'

'Really?'

'With the story thing,' she laughed. 'In every other way Tusia would still say you're a total pain. But with the stories now. You've got it.'

He shuffled on the seat beside her and looked down at the watch newly strapped to his wrist.

'The story is, elephants never forget,' said Brodie.

'I know.'

'I'll never forget,' she whispered.

Hunter smiled his answer.

The boat took them back to Kanton. Kahuna was waiting for them.

'It is good you were the ones who made the journey here,' he said quietly. 'Knights of Neustria must be tested in the fire.' He traced a ring deep into the sand. The waves curled up the beach but they did not reach what he had drawn. Kahuna gestured to them and they knelt beside him around the edge of the circle. They bowed their heads and, in the silence, the sun beat down on their shoulders like the blade of a sword.

'When you leave this place, you know that you

302

must continue to protect all that you have seen and learnt?' Kahuna added, 'That is the promise of the Knights of Neustria.'

Brodie felt as if she was going to burst with pride. That's what they were then, now. Not just those who hoped to be Knights. But actually part of a network of protectors that stretched back through time. The thought made her smile as they boarded the plane that was taking them back to Fiji.

Fabyan and Hantaywee had stayed with Jurek and Kirill. Hantaywee told them about Site Three. She told them about what the Suppressors did. She explained how Kerrith had let her go.

'She must have known,' said Hunter, sitting back in deep satisfaction after munching his way through a feast of sweet potatoes and breadfruit. 'Tandi, I mean.'

'Known what?' said Brodie.

'About Hantaywee being held captive. It must have been the thing she wanted to tell us, before she died.'

Fabyan's face clouded as the pain of lost weeks of knowing about his wife overwhelmed him, but Hantaywee squeezed his hand. 'Working out what she did made Tandi a target,' she said softly. 'The Suppressors knew what she knew.'

Brodie looked down at the floor. The Suppressors knew that. But they didn't know everything.

* * *

The news reports made everything clear. A state-owned boat caught up in stormy waters in the Pacific Ocean. Two government workers lost at sea.

Summerfield put down the newspaper.

In his time in the job, three of those who worked above him had been lost. The power of three great controllers snuffed out like candle flames. It made him feel uneasy. More than uneasy. It terrified him.

He had two choices really. That much was clear. He could ride it out. Hope he was recognised in any new promotions. Or he could do what his gut was telling him and get out of the Black Chamber now.

Summerfield looked out of his office window. He wasn't a man who coped well with heights. That had been true from the very beginning. Although ambitious, Summerfield had never been a brave man and he had the feeling that if he stayed, bravery would be essential.

The sky was greying. It looked like rain. He turned his back on the window, breathed in deeply and made his decision.

Tusia was barely consolable as they boarded a plane for London a few days later.

'We'll visit,' promised Kirill. 'We'll come see you

all at Station X.'

Tusia's skin was blotchy and her face streaked with tears.

'And you tell Mum and Dad we'll want a run out in the Matroyska when we get back,' laughed Jurek.

Tusia hiccuped and the awkward knowledge that her parents had given away the camper van to Team Veritas stopped her tears.

No one else joined them in business class. Fabyan knew they'd want to be alone. And besides, there was so much to catch him up with. So much to explain and talk through. It was a good job the flight took hours. And it was a good job they could take it in turns to share the telling of the tale.

'Was certainly quite an adventure,' said Sicknote, who'd taken a seat by the window.

He looked different somehow and for a moment Brodie wondered why. Then she realised he wasn't wearing pyjamas. It was true, the garish patterned shorts he'd picked up in the Fijian market were, if anything, even more conspicuous than his normal attire. But they suited him. He looked good. Relaxed even. And Brodie realised since the time on the island, she hadn't seen him take a gulp of his inhaler.

Smithies cast Brodie a glance, almost as if acknowledging her realisation. 'Think how much we've learnt,' he said. 'How much we've seen of the world beyond Plato's cave.'

Brodie considered this.

'We certainly saw the light,' said Mrs Smithies, and her face too was relaxed and unlined. 'Not just the shadows of suppression.'

'It was so beautiful,' added Tusia. 'How it all fitted together. Like a puzzle.'

'And how seeing the light,' said Sheldon, 'changed everything.'

Brodie rested her arm on a pillow and shuffled to make herself more comfortable. 'You know, I was thinking about that,' she said. 'And about a story I heard.' She left time for the groans, the clever comments from Hunter, the laughter even. But there was none.

'Go on,' said her granddad, his cheeks now full of colour. 'Tell us the story.'

'It's from the Bible,' said Brodie, 'and it's about this man called Saul. And he wasn't really a very nice man. But one day he saw a bright light. And it changed things for him. So much that he changed his name. He became someone else. His new name was Paul.'

'Like Paul the Patagonian giant?' said Tusia. 'The last man to know the language of Babel.'

'Pigafetta gave the giant the name Paul,' said Hunter.

Brodie was warming to her theme. 'It's odd because the name means "small and humble".'

'Weird name to give to a giant then,' laughed Sheldon.

'I know,' said Brodie. 'But maybe they chose it because he saw the light like a child. Because he remembered the language everyone else had lost.'

'The universal language. The one which joined us all together. And could make all things possible,' said Hunter.

'Universe,' blurted Brodie.

'Excuse me?'

Brodie was embarrassed. 'Well, the clue's in the name,' she said. 'Uni means one. Like your ridiculous one-wheeled cycle thing.'

'Erm, not so much of the ridiculous, please, B,' teased Hunter.

'And verse, like verses of a poem. Collections of words. Universal language means one way of saying things.'

Hunter obviously couldn't help himself. 'Sorry. I'm trying to be nice because of the whole injured-arm thing. And I stopped myself saying anything earlier, but really, Brodie. You and your stories and poems.'

Sicknote was watching them with what seemed like enjoyment. 'Oh, I don't know. I think her poems and stories have served us very well, Mr Jenkins.'

Hunter took a handful of peanuts and washed them down with a swig of orange juice.

'And I was thinking myself, about one of the poem quotes on the walls from the Library of Congress.'

Hunter nearly choked on his peanuts. 'Not you as well.' He looked a little sheepish. 'There were loads of quotes around that library.'

'This one in particular was from Tennyson,' continued Sicknote.

'Good old faithful Knight of Neustria and Cambridge Apostle,' said Smithies. 'Which quote were you thinking of?'

'*One goal, one law, one element and one far-off divine event to which the whole creation moves,*' said Sicknote. 'I don't know what poem it's from but it got me thinking that the one far-off event which affected all we did as a team could have been connected to Smithies' story of the Tower of Babel.'

'It's when people stopped listening to each other,' said Friedman, and the way he spoke made Brodie realise how much not being listened to still hurt him. 'It's when humans saw some stories as being more important than others.'

'And it's when "codes" first became a thing of power,' said Smithies. He pushed his glasses on to his forehead and Brodie knew he was weighing this thought. 'Codes are about control. About not letting other people in on secrets. About not sharing information with everyone.'

'And I suppose once the Suppressors had a taste for keeping secrets and gaining power, they moved on to wipe some stories from even existing,' said Granddad.

'So the Tower of Babel could be the event Tennyson was talking about. The event which changed the world,' said Mrs Smithies.

Sicknote laughed. 'And it took a team of has-beens and children to understand it. You've got to say that's kind of perfect.'

'Perfect,' confirmed Brodie. 'And the best thing is, we worked it out, not by looking at beautiful documents in pristine leather covers. We worked it out by reading the tatty, scruffy pages of MS 408.'

'And that's why,' said Smithies, 'we overcame the Director and the Chairman in their pinstripe suits and cuff links. And no one believed it could ever be done.'

Tusia rested her hand on the old man's arm. 'We did it though. We found Avalon and we found the truth. And the truth is, it's possible for people to live together fairly and for everyone to be heard. That's a pretty amazing truth we've found.'

Fabyan squeezed his wife's hand. 'So, that's what we've done. The question now, is do we tell anyone?'

No one answered. The only sound was the thrum of the engine.

'I'm not sure we do,' said Smithies at last.

'But it's the greatest discovery in the world,' blurted Sheldon.

'That's exactly why we don't tell people.' Smithies watched the faces of those all around him and Brodie knew his answer wasn't rushed or hurried. He'd thought this through. 'We don't tell what we've found and we protect what we know.'

'And what about MS 408?' said Hunter. 'The world has waited over one hundred years since Voynich found the book in Mondragone Castle. They've waited for a translation. For someone to break the code.' He was almost pleading with Smithies. 'Don't we tell people what it says?'

'No.'

Friedman's jaw flexed. 'The Knights of Neustria never did. So as the new generation of Knights, then neither do we. We keep the secret too.'

'But what happens,' blurted Sheldon, 'if other people try and translate MS 408?'

'We let them,' said Smithies.

'But what if they get it wrong? What if their

translation is different to ours?' Tusia was almost desperate.

Smithies thought for a while. 'That might happen. New people might hear the story and for them the code will break another way. The story MS 408 tells will be different.'

'But—'

Smithies was not to be interrupted. 'Maybe in years to come, someone will say they've translated MS 408. Maybe there'll be great rejoicing and worldwide attention.'

'What then?'

'It will simply be a different way of reading the universal language. Perhaps, at the time, it may seem logical and plausible. But,' he took a deep breath, 'the way we've read MS 408 is *true*. And truth is what matters.'

Brodie tried to make sense of all Smithies had said. 'So it comes back to allowing everyone to have their own story,' she said, and the way Smithies looked at her made her believe he'd never been more proud.

'I propose a toast,' he said, and he raised a glass of champagne in the air.

Brodie lifted her own glass of lemonade and giggled. 'To what?'

'To MS 408,' said Smithies, and his glass clinked against her own.

'We've travelled all around the world,' added her granddad, putting his own glass back on the table, 'and soon we'll be back at Bletchley where this journey began. And now we'll understand properly, what we've seen and where we've been.'

Brodie smiled at him.

His eyes were dancing.

'We've been to Avalon,' she said.


They waited until Christmas morning.

It was odd to be back in England, cold and wrapped up tight against the snow, after spending weeks in the warmth of the Pacific Ocean. They spent a while getting used to being home. To eating and sleeping and laughing. And to telling stories.

And then, on the dawning of the twenty-fifth, they got together to remember.

Thirteen people stood in a circle, around the monument to the Polish cryptographers in the grounds of Station X. The monument was made of stone. It was shaped like an open book. It seemed appropriate. Adam was there. He held on to Kitty and they stood in the circle with the rest of the team. The circle enclosed the monument. The open book at the centre.

Bundled up against the cold of morning, Brodie held a posy of Michaelmas daisies. They were her mother's favourites. That, too, seemed appropriate.

'You know, Michaelmas is a word which celebrates the victory of the archangel Michael over the powers of darkness,' said Sicknote. He was wearing a suit. His hair was tidy. His shoulders square and unstooped.

Brodie took one of the flowers and she put it down gently on the monument.

'And Michaelmas daisies are from the aster family,' said Hantaywee.

Brodie remembered the name of John Jacob Astor, who'd lost his life on the *Titanic*. She wondered if John Jacob Astor's story was the one Hantaywee was remembering.

But Hantaywee looked up towards a frosty morning sky. 'Aster means stars.'

Brodie turned the meaning over in her mind. Of course it did. Everything, every part of this giant puzzle had come back to stars. The phoenix constellation was at the centre of all they'd learnt. She remembered what Saraide had said to her as they'd talked in the castle. 'Avalon is like a pole star to people. A way of guiding them, to show what's possible.'

She put down the rest of the posy. The flowers splayed across the open pages of the book.

They'd chosen Christmas morning to remember those who'd lost their lives in the battle which had brought them all together. All the Knights of Neustria. All the Cambridge Apostles. Her mother.

They'd also come to remember Tandi.

'One of the fourteen,' said Hunter quietly.

Brodie didn't know what he meant.

'We began with the Firebird Code,' he explained.

Still Brodie had no idea what he was trying to say. And so her father reached inside his pocket and he drew out the crumpled paper they'd found right at the very beginning of their search. The paper flapped in the icy breeze. Friedman read the words aloud.

'Worthy alchemists of words,' repeated Hunter. 'We tried to be that. And I think perhaps we were.' His voice had a triumphant spark. 'The phoenix of power in her cloak of elfin Urim was Avalon, in the end,' he added. 'And the dragons were like the Suppressors, thinking they could fly higher than the phoenix. And here we are, on the dawning of the twenty-fifth. Thirteen of us. One of the fourteen given up to the task.'

How did he do that? Brodie marvelled. How did he work all that out?

'We were all rejected, B. All of us. For being too bright, too weird, too clever, too strange, even too old.'

*To the worthy alchemist of words,*

*It is my dying wish that you seek the*

*Phoenix of power,*

*in her cloak of Elfin Urim,*

*she who is wrongly considered to fly*

*lower than the rightful dragon.*

*Search $1^{st}$ on the dawning of the $25^{th}$.*

*Such a task requires 14 from the one the world*

*rejected,*

*Professor*

*Arthur Van Der Essen*

Mr Bray nodded appreciatively.

'But there were fourteen of us and one of those fourteen gave up her life.'

Brodie counted round the circle and her focus hovered where the circle began. A place left for Tandi. A place unfilled.

'Our whole journey is summed up in that very first code,' said Hunter. 'All of what we've done, contained in the Firebird Code.'

Brodie shivered but it wasn't from the cold. A thought was forming in her mind like steam rising from the story he'd told. 'But circles are important,' she said. 'Circles and completion were what made all the difference.'

Now it was Hunter's turn to look confused.

'What are you saying?' Her granddad rested his hand against her good arm.

'I'm saying, if Hunter's right and the start of our journey was contained in the Firebird Code, then so is the end.'

'The end,' said Tusia, her eyes narrowing as if she was trying to squeeze meaning out of what Brodie had said.

'If the Firebird Code contains the beginning of all we've done, then it must contain the end.'

Brodie remembered the time she'd stood in the office of the Library of Congress. She'd determined then that one day she would have a book-lined office just like that one. 'Our work isn't over,' she said.

'We know that,' said Hunter. 'We've talked about moving on.'

'But it's not over *here*,' she blurted. 'We may have found Avalon. We may have solved all the puzzles and the clues and broken all the codes. But the message of the Firebird Code didn't end there, did it? What we have left to do is to honour the sacrifice of Kerrith's final act. She gave herself up to keep Avalon safe and so we need to keep working.'

It was obvious no one was sure what to say. Sheldon looked blank. 'But we've done it, Brodie. We've broken the code. What more is there to do?'

'The final message,' said Brodie. 'The phrase added to the numbers with the Firebird Code.'

The paper in Friedman's hands flickered in the breeze. He looked down and he read. '*Handle with care.*'

'We've got to teach the language of MS 408 to other people,' Brodie said. 'OK, we might not be able to tell them we're teaching the language of the Voynich Manuscript. We might not be able to tell them about the location of Avalon. But we can share and teach the universal language the book of Avalon contains.'

'But how?' Brodie could almost see Hunter's brain whirring to make sense of her suggestion.

'By teaching people to listen to the language of those the world rejected. By helping people see things again through the eyes of a child. By teaching them the truth that children managed to do what adults had failed. To understand the code.'

Tusia's eyes showed at last she understood. Her hands were open wide like the pages of the stone book in front of her. 'There are so many stories out there which haven't been heard. So many stories which have been suppressed or changed.'

'And just because we've defeated the Suppressors once,' said Kitty, 'doesn't mean they'll give up. It doesn't mean that they won't still fight to make truth and stories disappear.'

'So now we've done what we came to do,' continued Brodie, 'it's our job to teach all the stories we can. And more than that, to show people how to find them hidden in patterns and numbers and songs.' She looked at the three friends who stood closest to her. All of them, still school age, but so much wiser than many adults she'd known. The friends who'd used the things they loved most to make all the code-breaking possible. Story, and numbers, and pattern and music. Four corners of the universal language.

Friedman moved from where he stood and placed

his arm protectively around his daughter's shoulder. 'The completion, then, is handling the truth of Avalon with care,' he said. 'Is that what you're saying?'

'If we can teach people the language of MS 408,' Brodie said, 'and keep working as a team to do that, then nothing in the world is impossible for people.'

'But can we really do that?' said Sheldon.

Brodie laughed. She pressed her unbandaged hand against the open book. 'I reckon we're the only people who possibly can!'

And so in that moment, though no more words were shared, a decision was made. An agreement reached.

Everyone would stay together at Station X, the home of the code, and they would work together, finding ways to help people reclaim and share stories.

Station X would become a centre for stories. A place, as it had been in the war, where truth could be revealed. It would become the place where the strength of Avalon burned strongest. And Team Veritas would work together to help others discover what they knew now to be true. That through song, and pattern and number, stories – important stories, forgotten stories, suppressed stories – could all be refound if they were handled with care.

But for now they stood in a circle around the open book of the monument. Sun streamed down on the ice-capped stone. Colours rippled below the surface.

And it looked for a moment as if flames of a mighty fire burned inside.

A fire, Brodie knew, which would never go out.

## TRUTH:

In the year 2012, Secret Breakers met together at Station X in Bletchley Park Mansion to try and decipher the Voynich Manuscript. All previous attempts to read MS 408 had failed.

Team Veritas, a collection of children and has-been code-crackers, made sense of the code.

They uncovered a secret history of a place where all people are valued, where every story is listened to, and where every voice is heard. They read the universal language of Babel.

'Codes' are about maintaining secrets and preserving power. 'Codes' are also binding rules of life. After careful consideration, Team Veritas shared the full extent of their discoveries with only a chosen few. You are one of the chosen.

In every generation, Suppressors will come to try and extinguish the fires of truth and possibility. Those with power will rank some stories and histories as more important than others.

The truth of MS 408 is the most important story of all time. Protecting that truth means keeping the Firebird Code and sharing what you now know with worthy alchemists of code.

And fighting for the right to share stories of all kinds from all peoples is what the Knights of Neustria pledged to do, and what all new Secret Breakers should continue to promise.

You have seen the truth. Now use the truth to set stories and people free.

# AUTHOR'S NOTE

## THE POWER OF LANGUAGE

For me, the deciphering of MS 408 was a way of exploring the amazing power of words. It's incredible to think that words can bring people together; make it possible to share emotions and perhaps, in some cases, be used to control. I love the bible story about the Tower of Babel and how in order to take their power away, God made people speak different languages. This created divisions and according to the story, the fabulous Tower of Babel was never completed because people could no longer understand each other. In *Secret Breakers* I wanted to explore the idea that if we try hard enough, there are some languages we can all understand: the language of music, the language of nature, the language of emotion.

And it doesn't matter where in the world you live or what words you use to speak, these languages are common to us all. The language of MS 408 was a language like this – one we could all understand if we fought hard enough to remember!

## THE POWER OF FIRE

Fire has always scared me. While writing *Secret Breakers*, I tried to understand whether fire was good or bad. It gives warmth and helps us survive, but it can bring great destruction and harm. Nearly every culture has a story about the stealing of fire. Some nations explain that Prometheus was the fire thief; others that Coyote took the flame. However the story is told, the idea of fire being amazingly powerful is made very clear in the telling. This connects to the idea that words too have exceptional power! They can be used to encourage and to help, or to humiliate or to scare. Lots of the reading I did as research for this series led me to think about fire as being a spark of imagination and just like real fire, imagination can be used for both good and bad. I hope that readers of *Secret Breakers* will use the fire of their imaginations to form diamonds ... and not to do harm!

# JOURNEY TO AVALON

At the very beginning of the *Secret Breakers* adventure I took inspiration from the myths and legends concerning King Arthur. MS 408 was always going to lead to Avalon. Stories of Avalon focus on its magic but as Smithies and Sicknote explain to the *Secret Breakers*, the real power of Avalon comes from belief in the potential that people can live well together. The symbol of the Knights' Round Table is key to the legends. A Round Table made of wood (a material which has the potential to store fire) where everyone is seated as equals, King and Knights alike. The idea of a sword of Avalon only belonging to one person troubled me. I wanted to explore this idea in the story of *Secret Breakers* and I decided that it was Arthur's belief in his ability that enabled him to pull a sword from a stone. *Secret Breakers* celebrates everyone's ability to do well given the right opportunities.

The hope of a Utopia like Avalon is explained as working like a pole star which helps people navigate forward. The codes led Team Veritas to the real Phoenix Islands and the aptly named Arthur Island. I was so excited to see the connection to the map page in MS 408 and all the links made to stars in previous instalments of the adventure. The Phoenix Islands really do sit close to the International Dateline and so time plays tricks here. A perfect place then to build a perfect society, hidden from the rest of the world.

# OTHER TRANSLATIONS OF MS 408

The world is still fascinated by Voynich's Manuscript. In 2014, just as this book was going to print, a professor from Bedfordshire University claimed to have made progress with the unread ancient book. Just like me, he believed the star pages were important to the translation. It's likely that over time, he and other researchers will make even more advances with the text. But as Smithies explains to Team Veritas, there may be many ways to make sense of the code that has baffled code-crackers for centuries. Other deciphering might lead to different interpretations but the truth of what Team Veritas discover will always remain.

# ANTONIO PIGAFETTA, MARTIN DE JUDICABUS AND HANS OF AACHEN

These men really were three of only eighteen survivors to complete the very first circumnavigation of the world. The details about Pigafetta's writing included in the story are true and a copy of his work, containing that map of nine unnamed islands, is really stored at Yale University, just like Voynich's incredible manuscript. One manuscript is beautifully presented; one is tatty and battered. In my imagination they work together to make sense of one amazing story of discovery and adventure.

# CIRCLE OF FIRE

The idea of the ring of fire was always important to me as I wanted my characters to come full circle in this adventure, having learnt more about language and about life. The *Secret Breakers* began their quest with the Firebird Code which led them to the universal language of music. In the final book they return to the idea of the Firebird Code and the importance of universal language and they promise that they will continue to work together uncovering and protecting stories that have not yet been heard. I hope you are tempted to do your best to keep the spirit of the Firebird Code yourself now that you have completed the journey to Avalon alongside the modern day Knights of Neustria.

# SECRET BREAKERS

## Discover the world of the Secret Breakers.

For more information about H. L. Dennis
and the Secret Breakers visit

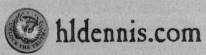 hldennis.com

You'll find competitions, code cracking lessons
and discover lots more secrets!

REAL CODES. REAL MYSTERIES. REAL DANGER.

Sign up for the Secret Breakers newsletter and get exclusive news, brand new code cracking activities and lots of behind the scenes information about each book!

 hldennis.com/mailing-list